Playing the Field

The Making the Play Series

By L.M. Reid

Published by
Scarlet Lantern Publishing

SCARLET LANTERN
Publishing

Prologue

Avery
Twelve years ago…

I hear yelling. My mom and dad fighting again.

Next comes the sound of glass shattering. My hands cover my ears as I slowly rock on my bed, praying for it to stop. The prayers never worked before, but I still hold out hope. The longer I sit here, the louder the sounds get. Louder. Scarier.

Tiptoeing to the bedroom door, I softly turn the lock.

I'm always afraid that he's going to come in my room. That he's going to take his anger out on me.

It doesn't happen every time. But it happens. And when it does…

I shake the thought out of my head and reach for my backpack. It's my escape pack. The one that I keep stocked with a book and snacks so I can go somewhere and hide safely. Luckily, the fire escape is in my room in this apartment, so my sneaking out is done safely with minimal chance of getting caught. I slowly lift the creaky old window up, just enough so I can squeeze through it.

We only moved here a week ago, but I already have my hiding spot staked out. There are two large bushes tucked away in the corner, and there is a big enough gap between them for me to be tucked away and out of view.

Settled into my new hiding spot, I pull on the zipper of my backpack and dig out my flashlight and my favorite book.

For the first time since I got home from school, I feel like I can relax a little.

"Who are you?"

The voice startles me, causing my body to jolt. My hands fumble, but after a few moments, I move my flashlight in the direction where the voice came from.

The voice screams at me to put my flashlight away at the same time I yell at it, "Go away."

"I didn't mean to scare you. I live here," the boy tells me. He moves closer, one hand trying to cover his eyes from the light. In his other, he's carrying a football.

"It's too dark to play outside," I tell him.

"It's too dark to… are you reading? How can you see?" he asks. I shine the light in his face again. "Hey, quit it."

He puts his hands in front of his face to try to keep the light out, and the way he's waving them around makes me laugh. For some reason, hearing me laugh makes him laugh too.

"I thought I was the only one that hid out here," he said.

"What are you hiding from?" I ask.

"My parents."

"Me too."

He points his finger at the ground in front of me. "Can I sit?"

I'm not supposed to talk to strangers, but I'm pretty sure my parents aren't supposed to leave bruises on me like they do either. He seems less scary than them, so I nod. We sit there for a moment, just staring at each other.

We may have just met, but the fact that we are both hiding from our parents tells us all we need to know.

The boy, whose name I still do not know, begins to speak. "Did something fall on you?"

I shake my head and look down at the ground. I was hoping in the dark he wouldn't notice, but the flashlight shined in just the right way for him to see.

"Then how did you get the bruises?" he asks.

His questions are understandable. Here I am in hiding in the bushes, in the dark, covered in bruises. I would be wondering the same thing if I were in his shoes. Still, I don't like his questions. They sound familiar, just like the ones that the social worker asks when she visits. As much as I hate the fighting and the hitting, the idea of the group home that she said I would have to go to sounds even worse. A place where I would have to live with other kids who have bad parents like me.

"I don't want to tell you," I say.

He pulls up the sleeve on his shirt. "I got this riding my friend Hunter's bike. I don't have my own bike, but when I go to his house, he lets me ride his."

"I didn't get them riding a bike."

It's almost as though he can sense that I'm uncomfortable. That whatever caused the bruises isn't good, and I don't want to talk about it.

He changes the subject by introducing himself. "I'm Mason. What's your name?"

"Avery." We just sit there quietly for a little while. "My dad."

"What about him?"

"He's the one that gave me the bruises."

"Why would he do that?" Mason asks.

I look at him strangely, curious as to why he is hiding from his own parents if they don't hurt him. But it's nice having someone to talk to and since I don't have many friends, I decide to let him in on my secret.

"I made him mad," I say. "I make him mad a lot."

"He shouldn't hurt you. That's not what parents are supposed to do."

"I know." I say a silent prayer hoping that one day it will stop.

"You're always welcome to come to my house if you need a place to hide. We don't have much, but no one will find you." His suggestion is sweet but makes me wonder even more about why in the world he would hide from his parents.

"What about your mom and dad?"

He shrugs. "They don't come around a lot. It's mostly me and my sister Quinn." He's quiet for a minute, then smiles. "Hear that car?" I nod. "That's them. They're leaving." He jumps to his feet. "So, you want to come inside? We have power this month, so the television is on. We can watch something."

I nod my head enthusiastically before following him back into the building.

"I live on the third floor," he says.

"I live on the fourth."

A soft "Oh" falls from his lips.

One single word. It's all he says, but I know exactly what it means. He's heard us. But he doesn't look at me with pity like other people do. He doesn't threaten to call anyone. Instead, he just opens the door to his home for me. When we step inside, we can hear the yelling above us. I look down at the ground shamefully.

"I'm sorry your dad's a jerk," Mason says.

"Thanks."

He moves further into the apartment and heads directly to the television. With the volume knob in his hand, he turns it up, drowning out most of the noise above us. He winks at me. "Have a seat. I'll get us a snack."

I sit in front of the television, my legs crisscross applesauce in front of me. Mason leaves the room, but I can hear him making noise. Things are banging and clanging together, followed by a loud "woohoo."

He walks proudly back into the living room with a smile on his face and a package of cookies in his hands. "We hit the jackpot."

He settles onto the floor next to me and hands the bag of cookies to me. "Have as many as you want."

I take one out of the bag. "Thank you. Where's your sister?"

"She's asleep." He shakes his head as he laughs. "One time, I jumped on her bed for five minutes, and she didn't wake up."

"I wish I could sleep like that," I tell him. The idea sounds so appealing. A simple way to drown out the noise that terrifies me.

He nods in agreement before turning his attention to the television. The show is in black and white about a family with a bunch of kids. They all seem happy, and the parents are so nice.

"I love this show," he says. "I wish someday I will have a family like that."

"Me, too."

"Do you have any brothers or sisters?" he asks. I shake my head. "Well, like I said. It's just my sister and me here most of the time, and I'm a really good brother. You can be part of our family too… if you want."

"Really?"

He nods his head and pops another cookie in his mouth. "Yep. And my friend Hunter, he helps us out. You'll like him."

"Cool," I reply as I grab for another cookie. Our hands touch and my cheeks instantly feel warm. I move my hand away and stare at the show.

I'm trying to remain cool, but inside I am bursting with excitement. I've never really had a friend before. I've always been afraid to, worried that they would stop liking me when they found out what my family was like. But not Mason. He gets it. He gets me.

We sit here, next to each other, our arms touching, trying to drown out the yelling from above with the sound of the television.

When it finally stops, I sigh. "It's late; I should go."

Mason jumps up and sticks his hand out to me. I look down at it, then back up at him. Putting my hand in his makes me nervous. So does the idea that if I don't, he might not like me. And I can't lose my first and only friend.

With my hand in his, he pulls me to my feet before walking me to the door. "If you ever want to come back, you can. You can come here whenever you need to."

I smile at him, then lean in and kiss his cheek. "Thank you, Mason."

He has no idea what this night means to me. Or, what's bound to happen when I return home if I'm caught.

His cheeks turn bright red, and he kicks his foot at the ground. "Night, Avery."

I sneak back into the same window that I snuck out of hours earlier. When I turn on the light to get myself ready for bed, I realize I am not alone.

My dad is standing there, leaning against the wall, his belt in his hands.

I know the drill.

I hate it, but I know it.

With tears stinging my eyes, I brace myself for what is about to come. The inevitable.

This time, when the bad starts to seep in, it isn't a place that I allow myself to drift off to. It's Mason. His face, his smile.

My friend.

Chapter 1

Avery

My arms are filled with grocery bags as I fumble for the key to Mason's condo.

He had a long day yesterday and practice later this morning, so I'm fairly certain he's still asleep.

The moans and screams that I hear as I step inside tell me otherwise. The sounds are deafening and send an ache straight to my chest.

When in the hell will I learn to knock?

My eyes fall to the keys in my hand.

"My home is your home. Always."

That's what Mason said the day he bought this place and handed me my own key.

You would think I would be used to this by now – Mason and all his women. After all, this isn't the first time I've walked into something I shouldn't have.

However, I definitely need to make sure it's the last. I can't keep doing this to myself. It's hard enough keeping these romantic feelings for my best friend from seeping in. Most days I can keep them at bay, just grateful to have him in my life. Days like today, though, they're torture. The idea of him with someone else is one thing. To have to witness it is a whole other ballgame of heartache.

For as jealous as I am that these women have a piece of him that I never will. At the same time, I also know that I have a piece of him that no one else will ever have – him.

Other women get the physical. Sex.

I, however, get everything else.

Every secret. Every nightmare. Every emotion.

There's history and secrets. Battle scars that no one else knows about but us.

Those pieces of him are mine and only mine. It makes me simultaneously grateful and angry. I get the best of him, but not all of him.

We know every single thing about each other. We need each other. It's that need that drives me to keep my feelings hidden. The crush I've harbored for him since college.

The loudest of the screams – his name falling from her lips – makes my ears ring as I set the groceries on the counter. The events transpiring make me cringe, but I know there is nothing I can do about it.

Knock, Avery. You could knock, I remind myself.

Except I never will. That key, it's symbolic of what sets me apart from the other women. Regardless of how pathetic it might sound, it makes me feel special knowing I have a piece of him that none of them ever will.

I can come and go as I please.

They, on the other hand, just come and then have to go.

Mason's lack of desire for a monogamous relationship is understandable. The life that he and Quinn, his sister, grew up with is unfathomable. The lives we all grew up in, really.

Abusive parents. Absent parents. Selfish parents.

That's what we had. What we were stuck with.

All three of us lacked anything resembling parentage. My parents, mostly my father, was an abuser. My mother was a broken and battered woman that eventually saved herself and left her daughter behind. And Mason and Quinn, well, their parents were never around. And when they were, the apartment looked more like a brothel than anything else.

So, we made our own little family.

Mason at the helm of it.

He took so much upon himself, deeming him the head of our "family," and it was his job and his alone to care for Quinn and me. He did, too. Despite not fully understanding what love was, Mason loved and cared for Quinn and me unconditionally. He took care of us. Worked hard to make something of himself – for us.

Mason has spent the better part of his adult life battling his fear of becoming his father. Believing he's already like him in so many ways, Mason always feared falling over the edge and becoming the man he despised. The man who didn't love his wife or children – only sex.

It's what led Mason to steer clear of relationships. They're something he avoids at all costs. Emotions, too. The more he drifted away from those emotional connections, the more and more he felt like his father. Like his path in life was set.

I wish he would realize how wrong he is. Despite my best attempts, nothing I have ever done or said could deter him from his way of thinking. Inaccurate as it is.

Aside from sharing the same smile and chocolate brown eyes, the two are nothing alike.

Mason may not see it, but he has the biggest heart of anyone I know. He's selfless. Always putting Quinn, Hunter, or me above everything else. His family. His people. That's what he lives for. From the charity he runs that helps raise money to provide underprivileged kids with college scholarships to the way he so generously donates his time to his alma mater through volunteer coaching and financial donations.

Even with all of those things, every amazing piece of himself, he still harbors the fear that underneath hides a monster, just like his father, that can come out at any moment.

"Can't I…" I hear a voice say. The woman's voice. It interrupts my thoughts and pulls me back into my own personal hell.

Her sentence is quickly cut off by Mason's abrupt, "No."

From my spot in the kitchen, I have a perfect view of him ushering her toward the door.

She's perfect. Model perfect. Long blonde hair to match her long, lean body.

"But Mason…"

"Sorry, gorgeous. You knew the deal." Mason does a double-take when he notices me in the kitchen. There's a slight smirk on his lips as he rolls his eyes.

The woman flips her hair over her shoulder and grabs the door handle. The "whatever" that falls from her shiny red lips indicates a completely different feeling than her overly flippant attitude. No, she's pissed. And probably even a little sad.

I feel her pain on that.

Mason is right, though. She knew what she was getting herself into. He is extremely open about him only having one love – playing the field. In football and in his personal life. If you can't deal with it, then don't step off the sidelines.

It's the sole reason why I've never told him how I feel. Why I never will.

My feelings, whatever they might be, won't be reciprocated. I know that. I'm okay with that. As okay as I can be, at least. Moments like these really test the strength of my heart. Deep down, I know it's for the best. I know that if I want Mason in my life that this is how it has to be. Life without Mason isn't an option.

There's a loud thud where I can only assume the woman slammed the door behind her. As emotionally frustrating as the whole situation is for me, I can't help but laugh. I've lost count of how many doors he's had slammed in his face and the countless times he's been slapped across the face. Yet, he still keeps diving back into the abyss of women.

"There she is," he says boastfully as he enters the kitchen. His arms instantly wrap around me in a giant bear hug as he presses a kiss to my cheek.

"Ew. Do not put your mouth on me. I do not know where it's been."

"Well..."

My hands press against his chest. "And I don't want to."

"Always such a prude," he teases as he grabs one of the apples I set on the counter.

"I am not a prude," I argue.

Just because I haven't had much luck in the dating department doesn't make me a prude. Really, it's his fault. How am I supposed to find someone who even remotely compares to the man currently on the opposite side of the island from me? The one that owns me, heart and soul.

"When's the last time you got laid?" he asks.

I can feel my cheeks flush, and I am certain they are a bright, fiery red. "None of your business."

I'm surprised I can utter the words. These are not conversations that we have. Yes, he runs his mouth about all of his random hook-ups, but that I'm accustomed to. We never talk about my love life or lack thereof.

In fact, I'm pretty sure he looks at me like one of the guys.

"You know when I did." His teeth dig into the red apple, a smirk on his lips as he chews.

"Yeah, I got to hear part of it, too. Thanks for that."

"At least you know the rumors are true."

Egotistical isn't a strong enough word to describe the man and how much he thinks of his sexual prowess.

I over exaggerate the roll of my eyes for effect. "Anyway, I'm sorry to have intruded…"

"You are never an intrusion, Ave. You know that."

"I stopped at the market this morning, and the fruit was too good to pass up. I over-bought, as usual, so I decided to drop some off on my way to class."

I grab my bag and lob it onto my shoulder.

"Leaving so soon?"

"Like I said, I have class."

"Oh, come on, Ave. Remember when we used to ditch school and spend the whole day in the woods drinking and hiking?"

A smile spreads across my face as I recall the exact times he's talking about. Those were the good days that we managed to somehow sprinkle between the bad. There, in the woods, just the two of us, everything was right with the world, at least for a little while.

"And you have practice in an hour," I continue.

"Shit," he says with a groan. "How do you keep my schedule and yours straight? I barely know what the hell I'm doing most days."

Because I know everything about you.

"Someone needs to keep you in line."

Mason leans against the door frame as I step through it. "You'll be at the game on Sunday?"

"I wouldn't miss it for the world."

Chapter 2

Mason

"So?" Ashton asks when I walk into the locker room.

"So, what?" I ask, even though I already know what he's getting at. My smile is answer enough.

"I hate you," he says, despite the fact that he's laughing.

I take it as a compliment since the guy is fresh out of college and already the Red Devils starting quarterback. He's an overly talented son-of-a-bitch. A God among Gods. And he hates me?

Good.

What started out as a friendly competition to see which one of us could land the girl turned into me needing to prove myself. To whom, I'm not sure. It doesn't matter for shit. I was, however, elated when the model picked me over him. And I fully intend on gloating about it this morning.

The only downside to the whole scenario was Avery having to witness me walking the woman out this morning.

Yes, it's a well-known fact that I'm a player both on and off the field. And I don't mind one damn bit that the world sees me that way. However, I don't like Avery seeing that side of me. Not up close and personal like that, at least. Yes, she knows. Better than anyone. The worst of it is that she knows the truth behind it, why I am the way I am. How every woman I'm with makes me more and more like *him*.

So, yeah, Avery might know it, just like everyone else, but for her to have to witness it?

Fuck, that damn near broke me.

And the look on her face?

A look of disappointment that's now ingrained in my memory. The look in her eyes that screamed I am better than that when I know with certainty that I'm not. Avery won't ever admit it though. Her ever positive attitude, despite the shit life we grew up with, always encouraging me and telling me that I'm not him.

Except, I am.

Anika is proof enough that Avery is wrong. Her and the long line of nameless women I leave behind.

Rather than dealing with it and risking explaining myself to Avery, I deflected and changed the direction of the conversation onto something else. Just like I always do. Only this time, I made the mistake of turning the tables onto her sex life. Bad idea. That only led to me thinking about her. Then about her having sex. Worst of all, or best depending on how you look at it, me having sex with her.

While I imagine it would be glorious, just the thought of it feels incredibly wrong.

Wrong or not, it's been the only damn thing I've been thinking about since she walked out the door.

Guilt eats at me. This is Avery I'm talking about here. My best friend. My family. She is the last person I should be thinking about as a sexual being. Fucking hell if I can turn it off now.

"Earth to Mason." Hunter's waving his hand in front of my face.

"Shit, you scared me," I say as I slap it away.

"What the fuck has gotten into you today? You've been standing here staring at your locker for ten minutes."

"I bet Anika sucked his brains right out of his dick last night," Ashton chimes in from the other side of the room.

"Fuck off, Winfield," I shout back to him. "And that was this morning for your information."

I give the woman credit; she was fucking dirty and willing to do just about anything I wanted her to. Why shouldn't I make Ashton eat his heart out a little more than he already is?

Hunter's eyebrows are raised, and he's staring at me. The asshole knows me too well. So well that there is no way I can sit here and lie to him. He'll see right through it, through me, and just keep pressing until he gets the truth out of me.

"Avery walked in as I was walking Anika out," I tell Hunter. I can see the hint of a smile peeking through. "Don't go getting any crazy ideas. I just don't want her to see that side of me."

"You sure that's all it is?" He now has a full-blown shit eating grin on his face.

"Yes, I'm sure. Christ, what the fuck is wrong with you and Quinn anyway? Where did you two get the stupid idea that I'm interested in Avery as anything more than a friend?"

"Oh, I don't know... maybe from watching you two for the past twelve years? No matter what, it always comes down to the two of you. You would do anything for each other."

"I would do anything for you, too, asshole. And if you think I want any part of your junk, you're fucking wrong."

"Tell yourself what you want Mase, we all see it." He shrugs his shoulders as if there is no way I can deny what he's saying.

"I do not want Avery," I say, my voice a little more frustrated and a little louder than it should be.

Trent chooses that exact moment to walk up. "That the hot little friend of yours that's always following you around?" Trent asks. "If you don't want her, I will definitely hit that."

The room goes silent. No one, and I mean no one, messes with Avery. I turn, my feet carrying my body in Trent's direction. "You lay a finger on her, and so help me God…"

Hunter's hands are on my arms, pulling me back. "He's just fucking with you. Let it go."

"Don't touch her," I warn Trent, who only laughs in response.

Trent Richards is the new defensive end signed to the Red Devils. And, for some reason, my nemesis.

The guy joined the team and instantly had a hard-on for me. I don't have a fucking clue why or what the hell I could have done to him since before he signed with the Red Devils, I barely even knew who he was. He's young, fresh out of college, just like Ashton. But, where Ashton really is a God in football, Trent merely thinks he is. Don't get me wrong, the guy is good. Way better than I would like him to be, in fact. Still, he's a total dick. And for some reason, he's gunning for me.

Every move I make, he's on me. Everything I say, he's got some smart fucking reply. Like now. Only, he doesn't know just how far he fucking overstepped. Because no one, and I mean no one, talks about Avery like that. Avery isn't some football groupie. She's different. She deserves better than any of these assholes in this room – especially me.

Hunter might be able to hold me back in the locker room, but the minute I step foot on that field, all bets are off.

Practice starts out well enough. Stretches then drills. Followed up by me tackling that douchebag Trent – hard.

The best part? I did it for no fucking reason. The play was over; I should have stopped.

Fuck that.

Fuck him.

"Oops," I say as I climb off of the now tackled defensive end.

When I glance over at Hunter, I'm surprised to find him laughing. I assumed he would be ready to give me that fatherly talk about how I need to keep calm. Blah. Blah. Blah. I shrug and chuckle a little as I head back toward the locker room.

"Hey, Mase, Coach wants to see you," Ashton calls out to me the minute I step through the doors.

Nodding my head in acknowledgment, I grab a towel and head to Coach Reed's office. He can rip me a new one all he wants; I don't even give a shit. Taking Trent down was worth any lashing that Coach can give me.

"You wanted to see me, Coach?" I ask innocently, pretending I don't know why he called me in here.

"Have a seat," he tells me.

Coach Reed and I might be close, but I've done my fair share to piss him off over the years, and that is definitely not his pissed voice.

If I had a mom or a puppy – I might be concerned here because it looks like one of them just died.

I drop into the seat across from him. "Listen, if this is about Trent…"

"How did you know?" he asks. His face is masked in shock and confusion.

"Because I knocked him on his ass?"

Coach Reed shakes his head as he settles back into his seat. "No, it's not about that. Listen, Mase, as you know, Trent is a great defensive player."

"He is. He's been working really hard all season," I agree. I may not like the guy, especially not now, but it's the truth.

"Good. I'm glad you agree. The organization wants to give him some play time, get him some more exposure," Coach tells me.

"I think that's a great idea." That part is most definitely a lie. The guy doesn't deserve shit. Not with his attitude. He needs to earn his damn spot, just like the rest of us did. Not get it handed to him on a silver platter.

"They want me to alternate the two of you. One of you would be the starter one week, and then the next week the other would start."

And there it is – I'm the fucking silver platter.

Son-of-a-bitch.

"What?" I exclaim. "You want to start him? Coach, he's good, but…"

"And he'll never get better if we don't give him a shot."

"A shot to what? Replace me?" I'm yelling now. At my coach of all people. Something I never in a million years would have done before this moment. This is a man that is the closest thing to a father figure that I have ever had. He means the world to me. Hell, I owe everything that I am to him. All the way back to my days at Remington University.

"This isn't an attempt to replace you, son. It's just that…"

"Just what? I bust my ass for you, and now you want to put Trent in my spot?"

"Mason, that's not…"

I shove out of the chair. "I don't give a fuck what you're trying to do. That's my spot. I have a contract. No way in hell are you replacing me. I won't let you."

I'm livid and furious that Coach Reed would even make such a suggestion. I started on this team. I worked my way up. I waited my turn. And since then? I've been busting my ass, killing myself to make sure not only I, but the entire team, succeeds.

I shove the locker room door open with enough force that it hits the wall behind it, the handle leaving a slight dent in the wall. They can take it out of my paycheck. The one I go onto that field and earn. Every. Fucking. Week.

"Hey," Hunter calls out to me. "Wait up."

Ignoring him, I continue on to my car.

He knows me well enough to know that something is wrong. And knowing him like I do, I know he's not going to give up until I tell him.

"Mason, what's going on? What did Coach want?" he shouts after me.

Anger gets the best of me, and I stop in the middle of the parking lot and face him. "You want to know? Fine. How about that he's going to be starting Trent. Fucking Trent. Not me. They want to give him some play time. Prepare him."

"Prepare him for what?"

"To be me when the season ends? How the fuck should I know?"

I do an about face and continue on to my car.

"That can't be right. You're the best in the league."

"Yeah? Fucking tell them that," I shout as I point back to the stadium.

I yank open the door to my car, Hunter's hand coming in and pushing it shut.

"What the fuck do you want from me?"

"I want you to calm the fuck down. I want you to quit being pissed and instead prove them wrong. They want to try and replace you? Show them why they shouldn't."

Knowing he's trying to help and wanting to hear it are two different things. I just want to be pissed. I damn well have every right to be. To be angry and fucking punch something. He's lucky it's not him.

Seeing that I'm not backing down, Hunter does. He steps back from the car. "Do what you want, Mase, but we both know that you showing up Trent on the field is going to be way better than any stupid stunt you pull."

Maybe. Maybe not.

Chapter 3

Avery

"Woah, where's the fire?" I ask when Mason storms into his condo.

His gym bag crashes to the floor with a loud thud. The vase that sat on the table next to the door crashes against the wall, glass shattering everywhere.

"Fuck," he screams out.

Anger and frustration radiate off his rigid body as he paces around the entranceway.

Without fear, I walk toward him. My fingers gently caressing his cheek. "What's wrong?"

"It's over." His voice is deep and filled with emotion as he says the words that make less than no sense to me.

"What is?"

"Me. My football career. All of it," he says as he pushes my hand away.

Moving past me, he heads straight for the wet bar and pours a drink which he downs with ease. And then another. "They want to start Trent."

"Okay..."

"They're trying to replace me, Ave. They want us to alternate starting weeks. They're looking to move me out."

"Coach Reed wouldn't do that to you," I say, knowing how much Coach adores Mason. They are more like father and son than anything else. There isn't a doubt in my mind that Coach Reed would never try to push Mason out. Not like this.

"Yeah, well, he just fucking did."

Mason's gripping the glass so tightly I'm afraid it's going to shatter in his hand. He begins to pace again, mumbling under his breath as he does.

"There has to be something else. Some reason," I say.

"Like what?" He's angry and shouting, but I know it isn't at me. "I'm playing my ass off. The season is going well. Where in the fuck is this coming from then?"

The truth is, I don't have a clue. Not even the slightest of an idea to suggest. None of it makes sense to me, and I'm sure that's where his frustration lies as well. All I can do is be there for him. Be his sounding board, someone for him to vent to. Someone to comfort him.

"I'm sorry, Mase."

My arms wrap around him, my head resting on his chest. The tension in his body slowly begins to dissipate as his arms wrap around me.

"I'm scared, Ave. I'm scared I'm going to lose it all."

"You won't," I say, trying to soothe the pain I know he's experiencing. Football is his life. It's everything he's worked for.

"You can't know that for sure."

"True. But what I do know is that no matter what, there is one thing that you will never lose."

"What's that?" he asks with a slight laugh. I'm sure he thinks I'm going to give him shit or make some joke about his collection of women.

That's not my intention at all. "You'll never lose me."

His arms squeeze a little tighter, and the feeling of him seeking comfort from me swells my heart a little bit more.

"Thank fuck for that. I don't know what I would do without you."

"Bang even more random women," I say, even though the words leave a bitter taste in my mouth.

"Probably. Which would probably result in me getting my ass kicked off the team even sooner," he says, dejected.

"Hey, even if for some crazy reason they did let you go, there are a dozen other teams out there that would be dying to snatch you up," I assure him.

It's a fact. He's a hot commodity in the football world. His heart, however, lies here in Remington. With the Red Devils. He and Hunter always dreamed of playing on the same team together. And I know leaving, not being on a team with him anymore, would hurt Mason, but he would be okay. I'm sure of it.

"Everything will work out, just like it's supposed to."

He laughs, just like he always does at my ever-optimistic attitude.

He presses a kiss to the top of my head.

The immediate anger and frustration subsiding, he makes his way into the kitchen. "How in the hell did you turn into Miss Positivity after how we grew up?"

I plop down on one of the barstools. "Things weren't so bad. We had some shitty parents. But I also had you and Quinn. And I am forever grateful for that."

"I'm the reason you're such a positive person?" he scoffs, unable to ever see the good in himself.

"You're impossible, you know that? You are one of the most positive and life-affirming people I have ever met. You have always championed for Quinn. And for me. Not to mention, Mr. Pro Football Player, you didn't exactly turn out so bad yourself."

"You want pizza for dinner?" He grabs his cellphone and begins to scroll.

"I'm serious, Mason."

"So am I. I'm starving."

Without another word, he orders the pizza and then heads to his room to change. He returns a few moments later, hoping that I had forgotten our earlier conversation. After all these years, you would think he would know better.

Flicking the television on, Mason settles himself onto the couch.

"You're not him, you know." I've told him this countless times.

Every time I get the same reply. "Thanks."

"One day, you'll believe me."

"Doubtful. But you keep on trying, Ave." There's a knock on the door. He rises from his seat and goes to get our pizza. "You know, you really should have been a cheerleader."

I've always been his cheerleader. Doesn't he realize that? Does he really think I won't keep trying to get him to see the man that I do? The one that took care of his sister and me? The man who volunteers his time to help other children in need. The man who donates money and schmoozes the elite just to offer a few scholarships to kids who need it?

He's selfless and kind. Yet all he sees, all he focuses on, is his abundance of women and lack of relationship with them. Not that he wants a relationship. He's been more than adamant about that. He thinks that makes him a bad guy, like his dad. If only he would realize that it's his decidedness in the fact that he's just like his father that makes him that man to begin with.

"I just wish you saw what I saw," I tell him when he sets the pizza down on the table between us. I grab a slice before settling back on the couch.

"You mean a rich, sexy football player?"

Yes, he is all those things. He's also so much more, though.

I make a play of choking on my pizza. Between the stuff with Trent and our conversation, I think the guy has had enough for tonight. I give him the reprieve and allow him to slip back into his comfortable persona. The ever cocky, always arrogant, football hero.

My hero.

My everything.

Chapter 4

Mason

My mind has been reeling since my conversation with Coach.

I can't help but feel like everything I've worked for is being taken from me. But why? For what? The team is doing great. I'm performing. What the hell is the issue, then?

And what the fuck is with Trent that he's gunning for me so badly? I've managed to resist kicking his ass so far, but he sure as hell isn't making it goddamn easy. He's everywhere. At least that's what it feels like. He comes after me on the field, in the locker room, and today even in the parking lot.

There has only been one upside to this entire week. That's been having Avery at my place every night when I get home.

Everything's been feeling tight lately, my body in overdrive as I try to out play someone years younger than me. Someone less battered and abused by the sport. Lucky for me, Aves is the best physical therapist there is. Even if she technically isn't one yet.

She's only two semesters away from making her dream come true and becoming a top-of-the-line therapist.

I just wish she would let me help her a little. Instead, she works, goes to school, and then essentially mothers my ass every day. The woman has enough on her plate, yet still makes time for me.

As much as I hate to admit it, I kind of like having someone to come home to. Who would have thought that the monotony of it all would be so appealing? Yet, here I am, at the end of practice looking forward to going home. To seeing Avery.

Maybe I'm just lonely. Sure, there are women, plenty of them. But having a woman in my bed for the night is vastly different than having someone to come home to. To share things with. It's not something I ever gave much thought to, but I like it, nonetheless. Liking it is irrelevant. I know how relationships go – they end. Usually, badly.

That's why I like things the way there are. Simple. Easy. Emotionless. No risk of hurting anyone. Or being hurt.

"Honey, I'm home," I call out in a singsong voice as I walk into my condo.

"Hey." Avery walks into the living room from the kitchen, and I stare at her. Gawk is more like it. The usual oversize tee shirt and leggings that she wears are gone and have been replaced with a short skirt and a pair of boots. The tank top she has on a little tighter than what she normally wears.

"Uh…" I stutter out the single sound. It's all I can muster because holy hell, what is going on here.

Avery looks amazing. Stunning.

"Did I miss the new stretching attire memo?" I ask, trying to appear confused, which I am, instead of turned on. Which I also am.

"No, but you must have missed the text from Billy inviting all of us out tonight," she says as she flashes her phone in front of my eyes.

Billy Saint went to Remington University with us but got drafted to the Wisconsin Jets. It was kind of a letdown. Billy's a good guy. Good ballplayer, too. And the two of us can definitely stir some shit on and off the field.

I should have known he would be reaching out. We're playing the Jet's this Sunday, so of course, he's in town. And every time he's in town, we get together. Why he felt the need to loop Avery in on this as well, I have no fucking clue. There's no backing out now, though. Avery is dressed and ready to go.

One last glance at her sexy as sin legs as I walk past her. "I'll be ready in ten."

*****

Billy is in rare form tonight. He's being funny and charming, and it all seems to be directed at Avery. And Avery, well, she seems to be eating it up.

If I didn't know better, I would think that he was flirting with her. Billy wouldn't do that. Billy knows better. He knows that Avery is off-limits. Even to a decent guy like him.

Avery was raised in a house with an abusive father and a useless mother. The shit life she grew up in isn't something she ever needs to relive. No, Avery deserves a good man. A man that's going to treat her with the respect that she deserves. The last thing she needs is some asshole football player who is going to be on the road doing God knows what. She needs a good guy, a nice guy. One who will give her the life she deserves.

So why in the fuck is she smiling at Billy so much?

A better question is, why in the hell is it bothering me so much? In ways that I don't understand. Ways that make me find the need to excuse myself from the table.

I'm standing at the bar, confused by whatever it is that I'm feeling.

Yes, I've always been a little overprotective, that I already know. But this? This is borderline fucking jealousy, and I don't have a clue where it's coming from.

Billy walks up beside me. "Everything alright? Not quite living up to your reputation tonight."

"You are," I grit out. I instantly regret the decision to call him out, because right as I do, Hunt walks up. If I say what I want to say to him – warn him away from her, Hunt will start in on his ranting about how much I secretly want Avery. I hear the shit enough. I don't need to hear it tonight. "Just… treat her right."

"Treat who right?" Billy asks. "Avery?" Billy shakes his head. "No way. I love Aves, but no way in hell am I laying a finger on your girl."

"You've been touching her all night." So much for denying it. The words slip out before I can stop them. Even I can hear the twinge of jealousy in what I just said. Fucking hell. Her and that skirt.

Hunter laughs, and I throw a glare in his direction. One that only makes him laugh more.

"Fuck both of you." I down the drink in my hand and set the glass on the counter.

Billy makes his way back to the table, scooting his seat a little further from Avery. I want to say he's an asshole for acting like that, but part of me is glad he moved. At least until I see Avery toss her head back in laughter at something he said.

Desperate to get Avery off my mind, my eyes scan the bar. I'll show Billy just how damn well I can live up to my reputation. There's a blonde woman sitting in the corner. She's alone. No date in sight. The perfect play.

I urge my feet to move, to carry me in the direction of the woman. A woman who can save my soul and my mind from getting wrapped up in something that I can never have.

Except that she doesn't. Not even in the slightest. Not even when she catches me watching her and flashes me those come fuck me eyes. Sexy as it might be, it doesn't hold a candle to the smile that Avery gave me earlier. The same one she's given me all these years that somehow now has my balls tightening and my dick begging for her and her alone.

"You good?" Hunter asks as he eyes me curiously.

I look back at Avery and Billy for a moment, carefree and having fun.

"Yeah, just tired. I'm going to head home."

"Alone?" Hunter asks.

Yep. I'm going home alone.

Chapter 5

Avery

Watching Mason on the field is like watching poetry in motion. He exudes pure athleticism. Every move, every tackle is strategic and precise.

"Oh, come on," I yell, jumping out of my seat.

The minute I took my seat, I was on the edge of it. I always am when I watch him play. A combination of pride and fear coursing through my veins.

Every play is a risk, a potential injury.

Something I would like to avoid seeing at all costs.

As I watch him exit the field, his walk a little stiff, I wonder if he did the pre-game stretching program that I gave him. He's been pushing himself extra hard all season. Especially since Trent Richards joined the team.

Then Coach Reed and the Red Devils organization decided to start Trent. That only sent Mason over the edge. He pushed himself harder than I have ever seen him push before. I'm not sure if it's the fear of being replaced by Trent or just a fear that Trent could be better.

God knows, for as arrogant as Mason might appear, deep down, he's anything but. He's worked doubly hard his entire life to prove himself. Mostly to himself.

Fear of being like his father, the wretched man that he was, fuels everything Mason does. Except for the women. For some reason, that's the one thing he held onto, the one thing he thinks seals his fate for being just like the man he despises.

With all the added pressure, and training, I was afraid that his muscles would be too tight, and he would pull something. Or worse.

I vowed to protect him, just like I always do. I made him my special project – my own personal internship of sorts. I researched every program available to man. I narrowed them down based on the stature of the person using them – same build, same stature, same muscle density. Once I weeded that out, I searched through each one looking for the program that would best suit his needs.

None of them did.

Instead, I created my own. I took all the best stretches. Anything that would optimize every single muscle in his body. After all, I know every damn inch of him. I knew what was tight, where he lacked in strength – not that he would ever admit that part. I knew because this has been our routine since high school. He works on his skills, and I ensure his body works properly to use them.

As I sit here now, I can only hope that he used it.

"Yes," I scream, jumping up again. Mason just took down Billy allowing for the wide receiver to score the much-needed touchdown. Even though we were already in the lead, any leeway helps. With the clock running, we're close to sealing the deal on this game.

Quinn grabs my arm and drags me back down to my seat. "Relax, will you," she says with a laugh.

"You know I can't do that," I say, scooting to the edge of my seat once again. My elbows rest on my knees as I lean forward as though those few inches somehow give me a better view.

Both of us have our eyes glued to the field. It's down to the wire. All they need to do now is run the clock down. My eyes bounce between the field and the clock, each moment seeming to tick by slower and slower until finally, it reaches zero.

I jump out of my seat, pulling Quinn with me. We jump, hug, and then escape our seats so we can find the guys before they hit the locker room.

I flash my pass to whoever tries to stop me as we make our way back to the locker room entrance.

"Don't even think about it," the security guard, Ralph, says. His gaze is directed at Quinn.

"What?" she asks innocently, batting her eyelashes at him.

Ralph just folds his arms across his chest and stares her down. Clearly, the only man on the planet that can resist Quinn's overt sexiness.

"Exactly what have you and Hunter been up to in the locker room?" I tease. Though, based on the look on Quinn's face, I'm not far off base.

With a pout, Quinn turns and rests against the wall next to me.

"He's acting like Hunter minded," she says, with a roll of her eyes.

"I do not want to know," I tell her.

"Oh, please, if you would quit lying to yourself and finally make a play for Mason, you would be doing the same thing," Quinn says, calling me out on the secret crush I have on my best friend.

Okay, maybe it's not so secret to Quinn. Or even Claire, Quinn's best friend and our other roommate. But to Mason? God, love him, but he doesn't have a clue. Thank goodness for that.

For whatever these feelings I'm having – been having – are, they aren't worth ruining my friendship with Mason. Despite Quinn's good intentions, she knows as well as I do that pursuing anything with Mason will only serve to destroy what we have built. I refuse to do that. I rely on him too much; I love him too much. That's why I made the decision long ago that Mason and I were friends, and that is all we will ever be.

It's not as though he has ever looked at me as anything but, anyways. In his eyes, I look no different than... Hunter. I certainly don't meet the criteria of the women he associates himself with. The perfect example being the woman he escorted out the other day. Tall, lean – perfect. I'm much curvier, more filled out. Ordinary. I don't fit the runway model look he usually goes for.

Even if I did. Even if he were interested...

Using my elbow, I jab Quinn in the side. "Keep your voice down."

"I'm just saying..."

"I know what you're saying, Quinn. And you know as well as I do that it doesn't mean a thing. Mason, he's not interested in me, or anyone else for that matter. Not like that, at least."

While we all grew up in abusive households that lacked parental love and supervision, we each walked away with different ideologies from it.

Where I still believe in real love and crave the feelings that I missed out on as a child, Mason revolts against it. He doesn't believe in love – not the romantic kind anyway.

In fact, he's so against it that he's never even so much as had a woman in his life that last more than a few dates, except Quinn and me.

It's something that makes me simultaneously grateful and sad. Sad for him and the life, or lack thereof, that he seems to believe he deserves and so grateful that I haven't lost him to another woman. Or, for that matter, had to stand by and watch him with one.

"Mason is just scared. Maybe if you…"

"No." My eyes find hers and implore her to shut up because just a few feet from us are Mason and Hunter.

They're both sweaty and dirty and grinning from ear to ear.

"We won, baby," Mason shouts. The term of endearment is most certainly not directed at me, but the open arms he charges at me with are. They scoop me up and squeeze me tightly.

"Congrats, Mase," I say as I hug him back.

He sets me back on the floor and shakes his head as he watches his best friend and sister kiss. "This shit's getting old. Get a room already," he tells them.

"You're just jealous," Hunter chides.

While I know Mason isn't, I sure as hell am. I wish someone would look at me the way that Hunter looks at Quinn. My sigh is soft because I'm also silently wishing that person was Mason, even though I know that I shouldn't be.

"Hey, Avery," a deep, gravelly voice greets me. Mason's arm is still around my shoulders as one of the other players, Trent, approaches us. "You look gorgeous."

My cheeks instantly blush at the compliment. How could they not? Trent is a stunning man. Tall, dark, and handsome. The fact that he called me gorgeous makes me a little happier than it should. And it shoots my confidence through the damn roof.

Before I can respond, I feel Mason's arm drop from my shoulders and his body disconnect from mine. I watch as he continues to move forward until he's toed to toe with Trent. "Back off."

Trent ignores Mason's warning, his eyes looking over Mason's shoulder to me. "The team's going out to celebrate tonight. I hope you're going to join us."

"Walk away, douchebag," Mason says.

As much as I don't want to, I remain silent. I don't need to make this little pissing match any worse than it already is.

"I'll save you a dance," Trent tells me with a wink.

Once Trent has moved out of sight, I give Mason a slight shove. "What the hell what that?"

"You are not getting involved with him," Mason deadpans.

The fact that he is giving me an order, telling me who I can and cannot date, has me furious. "What gives you the right to tell me who I can or cannot date?"

While I realize that Trent is going to be some major competition for Mason this year, there is no reason that I can see that I shouldn't accept Trent's offer. Trent moving up on the roster isn't his fault. It was the organization's decision, not his. Besides, he seems like a nice enough guy. And he is definitely hot as hell.

Why shouldn't I save a dance for Trent? Have a little fun? It's not like Mason hasn't had his fair share. Not once have I ever said a word about it to him. He sure as hell has no right. Besides, wasn't he the one taunting me the other day about the last time I got laid? Maybe it's time I narrow my timeframe a bit.

With my hands on my hips, I stand here dying to hear his response. His eyes are on me, but they won't meet mine. I can see the media coming into sight, which means that I'll have to wait for my reply. It's showtime for Mason, Hunter, and the rest of the team.

"We're going out tonight," Mason says as he pushes the locker room door open. "Head to my place; we'll meet you there."

Still irritated with his behavior, I give him a slight smile before turning my focus back onto me, onto my life. He's out living his. Why shouldn't I live mine? And who in the hell gives a damn if he likes it or not?

"Ave? You coming?" Quinn asks, as I stand there staring at the door to the locker room.

In that moment, I decide that I am. Hopefully, at the hand of Trent. Or whatever part of him he wants to use.

"Damn right I am," I say with a smile as I walk past her.

"I'm sorry, what?" she shouts as she follows me out of the stadium. Her voice is a mixture of confusion and excitement.

Admittedly, I'm a little of both, too. Frustrated by my feelings for Mason and irritated by him thinking he can tell me what, or who, to do, I decide to give him a taste of his own medicine. His actions and disappearing act last night were bad enough. Now this?

It's time I quit worrying about Mason and start having a little fun. And if I just so happen to make Mason suffer in the process? So be it.

"Who in the hell does Mason think he is anyway?" I continue on as we step into our apartment.

Quinn and I made a detour to our apartment to change and pick up Claire.

The entire car ride here, Quinn pried and questioned me. Each question was met with silence and a smirk because I know her, and I know exactly what she was thinking. That this has to do with Mason. And while, to a degree, that might be true, it's not in the way she is thinking.

At the end of the day, this is about me and what I deserve. I am not going to sit around and pine for something that's never going to happen. So why not enjoy what's interested and right in front of me?

When I step out into the living area with my black dress and red heels, I'm greeted with a very disappointed look on Quinn's face.

"What?" I ask. I glance down at my dress, trying to see what her issue with it might be.

"Nothing. You look… nice."

Something tells me in Quinn's book, nice doesn't actually mean "nice."

Claire steps out of the kitchen and chimes in. "I thought you were trying to get laid tonight?"

The question is telling enough of what she thinks of my current outfit. I throw my hands in the air, exasperated at the fact that apparently, I have not a clue as to how to dress. "Ugh, fine. Dress me, fix me, do what you want to me. Just make it quick, so we're not late."

Chapter 6

Mason

"Avery," I bellow as I step into my condo.

The place looks empty despite the ladies having left the stadium long before us. They should have been here by now.

Wherever they're at, I hope they hurry. I'm so pumped. I need to get out and burn off some of this excitement. That win felt so damn good. I'm filled with energy and feel more alive than I have in months. First, sticking it to Billy Saint. And showing up Trent made it all that much better. I glance down at my phone; there is a text from Billy telling me I'm an asshole, making me laugh.

Billy and I like to compete. On and off the field. Unlike things with Trent, Billy isn't gunning for me. Or my spot on the team. It's a friendly rivalry. Now, if only I could get both of them to understand that Avery is off limits. Don't get me wrong, Billy's a good guy. It's just that Avery, she deserves...

What Mason? What does she fucking deserve? Better than Trent, that's for sure. The guy is a player. And coming from me, that says a lot. The fact of the matter is most of us are except for a few guys, like Hunter. But again, that's a few. A rarity in the league. Most of us are still young and assholes enjoying the money, fame, and women that come along with it. Nowhere near ready to settle down.

Some of the guys try to fool themselves. They think they're in love, get married, and then bam – they're cheating. Not me though. I saw the truth at an early age.

The fact that very few men can even bother to keep it in their pants for the sake of love. I saw it with my parents. The random hook-ups and who knows what else. So many men and women both walking in and out of our apartment. I can still hear the sounds – screams, moans.

To this day, I don't know if they did that shit for fun or if it was some kind of business that they ran. All I knew was that I didn't want any part of that life. No love. No marriage.

I shake my head. The thought of my mostly absent parent's sex life traumatized me enough as a child. It's the last thing I need to be rehashing. It is no wonder I'm so fucked up.

Thinking of my parents always leaves me feeling dirty and tainted, so I jump in the shower to wash off the stench of my past.

A shower, a clean pair of clothes, and I feel back to normal. Or, at least, normal for me.

When I step into the living room Quinn and Hunter are sitting on the couch with Claire, who is currently arguing with Ashton. Avery is nowhere in sight.

"Where's Avery?" I ask.

"Right here," she says.

She steps casually into the room as if it's just another day when it's anything but. Not with her looking like that. If I thought the damn skirt and boots that she wore the other night was a turn on, it's nothing compared to what she looks like now.

Stunning.

Downright gorgeous.

My eyes widen as they take in every delectable inch of her body.

Holy hell.

Who is this woman, and what has she done with Avery? Because this sure as hell can't be her. Not in that dress, with those curves. The red satin of the dress hugging her body like a glove, a very tight, very sexy glove.

I blink my eyes, trying to rid myself of the visual and the sexual stirring that the sight of her is instilling in me.

This is Avery.

I shouldn't be staring at her like this.

I sure as hell shouldn't be thinking the very dirty, very inappropriate things I'm thinking right now either.

"Mason? You okay?" she asks.

"What? Yeah. Huh?"

There's a snort from the couch, my sister's laughter emerging. "Cat got your tongue, big brother?" Quinn taunts me. There's a Cheshire grin on her most definitely not innocent face. Only she would call me out like that in front of everyone. Especially Avery.

I clear my throat of the giant lump that has formed in it. "Let's go. The limo is waiting."

Allowing Avery to step before me, my hand falls to her back for the briefest of moments as we walk to the door. Soft, warm skin.

Want. Need.

My hand recoils from her back, the feel of her skin against mine way too tempting. I tell myself to back away to put some space between us. When we step into the elevator, I do the complete opposite. I stand next to her. Close to her. Way too close to her.

Unable to resist the urge, I dip my head and whisper into her ear, "You look amazing."

Her cheeks flush a deep red that almost matches her dress, and her eyes drop to the floor. "Oh, uh, thanks."

I go to say something else, but I draw a complete blank. The damn woman has left me speechless. Something that I rarely ever am. Especially not when it comes to women. I have every line, every come on, down pat. I can make women fall at my feet. Not this woman, though. Avery is different. She's a forever kind of girl when I'm a one-night kind of guy.

"You're welcome," Quinn says as I watch Avery slide into the limo.

"What exactly am I supposed to be thanking you for?" I ask her, my eyes still on Avery.

She glances at Avery and then back at me before sliding in next to Hunter with a satisfied smirk on her face.

Does she really expect me to thank her for torturing me? Because that is exactly what Avery looking like that is doing to me. It's turning me on in ways it shouldn't. It's making me consider things that I can't. It's making me want the one person I can't have. Avery, she deserves better than me, better than some fling. Because that's all I can offer her. Or anyone, for that matter. I'm nothing more than a good time.

When I slide in the limo next to her, my eyes immediately drop to her legs, the tan skin that looks like silk as she uncrosses and then re-crosses them.

Fucking hell. Is she trying to kill me here?

Everyone's laughing, drinking, and having a great time. Everyone except me. My hands are clasped in my lap, my leg bouncing in place as every ounce of my restraint is tested.

I feel her hand on my leg, the muscles instantly tense and still. "You're making the whole car shake," she says with a laugh. A soft, sexy laugh.

Jesus Christ, help me. "Sorry."

"You okay, Mase?" she asks. I glance down to where her hand is still on my leg. I am not okay, far from it. But I lie to her, tell her I'm fine and divert my attention to the passing buildings outside the window.

The moment the limo pulls up to the club, I throw the door open and bolt to the entrance. Thankful the bouncer recognizes me and unhooks the rope. I rush into the club and straight to the bar. I have tunnel vision, alcohol; I need it now.

The whiskey the bartender pours goes down smooth. So does the one I drink immediately after.

"Mason?" It's Avery's voice in my ear. The sound of my name falling from her lips has me on the verge of needing another drink.

"Yeah?"

"Are you sure you're okay? You seem a little off tonight." Of course, she notices. The woman knows me better than I know myself most of the damn time.

"I'm fine, really. Just on a bit of a high with the win tonight," I lie to her.

She opens her mouth to say something, but we're interrupted.

"Well, well, well." The sound of Trent's voice instantly grates on me and has me flagging down the bartender for another drink.

"Fuck off," I say.

"Not interested in you, Ford." When I glance in his direction, his eyes are on Avery, taking in every delicious piece of her – just like I did. "Hello, gorgeous."

"Hi, Trent." Avery's voice has this hint of sensuality to it. The smile on her red, plump lips making my cock twitch in my pants, despite the fact that the smile is intended for another man.

She's got to be kidding me with this, right? She's interested in this douche?

"Did I not make myself clear earlier today?" I grit out the question.

"You did. What you fail to realize, Ford, is that I don't give a fuck." He refocuses on Avery. "Dance with me?"

We're both staring at her awaiting her response. Don't do it, Ave. Don't do it.

"I would love to," she says as she slips her hand into his.

She would love to? Are you fucking kidding me?

My eyes never leave her as I watch her follow him to the dance floor. There's a fucking array of emotions that are running through me. Betrayal. Jealousy. Desire. I don't know where in the hell they're coming from or what the fuck I'm supposed to do with them.

What in the hell does she want with him anyway? The guy is a player at best and my fucking nemesis at worst. He can't give her what she needs.

And why is he focusing on her? Earlier today, and now? Women flock to his sorry ass. He can have any damn girl he wants and has made a point of doing exactly that. So why is he focusing on her? Why my Avery?

My Avery.

Jesus Christ, I can't believe I just phrased it that way. That damn dress of hers has me losing my mind.

So, yeah, I get why he's interested. Why he's focusing on her. She's fucking stunning. But still – she's mine. As wrong as those words sound, and even though I can't have her. He sure as hell can't have her either. I won't let him.

What do I do though? How in the hell do I stop this from happening?

She's tossing her head back in laughter; his arm is wrapped around her waist. His mouth is near her ear. They're having fun. And the idea of her having fun with him infuriates me. Just like it did last night when we hung out with Billy.

I'm no fool. I know she dates. I know there have been men in her life, but still, I can't think of a single time that I've seen her with someone else. For as much time as Avery and I spend together, countless nights just like this, she's never danced with anyone but Hunter or me. She's never gone home with someone. She's never not been mine.

And I hate it.

Hunter steps up next to me. "I definitely did not expect that," he says.

"What?" I ask dryly.

"Avery. In that dress." He lets out a slight chuckle. "Damn."

That makes two of us. Still, I throw him a look that screams for him to back off. Another possessive caveman move on my part. A source of amusement on his. Not only would he never hit on Avery, he's head over heels in love with my sister. My warning is pointless. Directed at the wrong person.

Trent doesn't seem to be listening, though. If he had been, he would know to stay away from Avery.

Everything about her is turning me on and infuriating me at the same time.

"You okay, man?" Hunter asks.

"Why does everyone keep asking me that?" I shout, finally losing my cool.

"You just seem a little… off your game tonight," Hunter says, with a chuckle.

"Me? Off my game?"

Hunter shrugs.

I'm not sure what he's trying to do here. Push me to Avery – or away from her. I find myself feeling the need to prove him wrong. To prove to him that I don't belong with Avery and that she can do better than me.

I scan the room, my eyes narrowing in on three blondes huddled together who have been checking me out all night.

"I am never off my game. I am the king of playing the field," I say, scoffing at his comment.

"Watch out, Mason Ford is on the prowl," Hunter says with a laugh.

I glance over to the blondes, then back to where Avery is standing with Trent.

"Damn right I am," I say as I take a step forward.

Only I don't step toward the blondes that I had set my eyes on. No. I move in Avery's direction. Determination in every step. Claiming her. Showing Trent exactly who Avery belongs to.

Me. Not him. Never him.

The feel of my hand gripping her arm has her head whipping in my direction. She doesn't have to speak, but I can already see the question in her eyes asking what in hell I think I'm doing?

It's the same question I am asking myself. This is Avery, and here I am staking a claim on a woman I can't be with. It's not fair to her.

I stare at her for a beat before Quinn grabs my attention and my arm. "Excuse us." She begins to pull me away. "Whatever you're about to do, don't." I'm ready to argue, but she continues on. "It's one thing to be a protective friend; it's another to act like a jealous boyfriend when you don't want to be one. Or do you?"

Hearing the term boyfriend, my eyes glance back at Avery. A boyfriend. That's what she deserves. Not me pulling some juvenile bullshit because someone else is playing with my toy. Avery isn't mine to claim. She never will be.

"Why don't you just admit it?" Quinn continues on as she leads me back to the bar.

"Nothing to admit," I tell her.

There isn't. Nothing more than an unexpected, inexplicable attraction to my best friend. Just because an overwhelming desire to fuck her has come over me – that doesn't make this anything.

It can't be anything.

Chapter 7

Avery

My focus should be on the man beside me. The one that's attention is fully on me.

Instead, my mind is on Mason. Like it always is.

There's something off about him tonight. I'm not sure what it is, but it started long before Trent interrupted our conversation. It started the moment he laid eyes on me.

I tried to talk to him, see if I upset him or if something happened that I wasn't aware of. Because he sure as hell sounded okay until he laid eyes on me.

Maybe all of this does have to do with Trent. Maybe Mason hates the guy more than I realized. It would explain why he marched over here half an hour ago and took my arm, looking like he was about to drag me out of here like a caveman.

"Want to get out of here?" Trent asks. His arm is wrapped around me, and his hand is resting on my waist. His lips are near my ear, his words a private invitation.

That's the million-dollar question, isn't it? Do I? Do I really want to go home with Trent? Have sex with him? Yes, that was my exact intention tonight. Enjoy myself, have sex with Trent, and stick it to Mason all at the same time.

Something's wrong though. Mason, he doesn't act like this. His attention is on me, not seeking out the woman of the day like it usually is. I'm fairly certain it's because of Trent. Because he hates him. Because he doesn't trust him. While his behavior at the stadium early today was completely unacceptable, suddenly, the idea of going home with Trent doesn't seem as appealing.

Trent repeats the question. This time, after he asks, he presses his lips against my neck. The implication behind the kiss more than obvious. Out of the corner of my eye, I see movement in the form of Mason stalking toward us. His body is stiff, his hands clenched at his sides. Quinn is beside him, begging him to stop.

To stop what, though? What in the hell is he doing?

"Mason don't," Quinn warns him.

He doesn't heed her warning, though. He storms up to where Trent and I stand, "We're leaving." Mason's words are an order. Just like they were earlier. Only this time, they don't infuriate me; they turn me on.

His hand grabs mine and pulls me out of Trent's hold and into his arms. Mason throws a glance in Trent's direction, a smirk spreading across his handsome face. His fingers lace with mine as he leads me out of the club and into the night.

There's an intense look in Mason's eyes that I can't quite read but know that it's significant, nonetheless. That look has me nervous and confused. Terrified and exhilarated. I don't know what's happening, but I love it all the same.

He gives the driver my address before sliding into the cab next to me. He doesn't speak, not a word, just stares at me. I'm at a loss, taken off guard by his abrupt change in behavior. I continue to remain quiet because I don't have a clue what to say.

My thoughts are all over the place. Part of me excited at what the possibility of this might mean. Another part of me trying to temper the excitement I feel because I know Mason, and I know that whatever this is, it's not permanent. It can't be. Mason doesn't do permanent.

His phone begins to chime and ring. I want to ask if he's going to see who it is, but the intense look on his face keeps me silent.

When the cab rolls to a stop in front of my building, he doesn't move. He doesn't even look at me. Still unsure of what in the hell just happened, I slide out of the cab. A second later, I hear the sound of a car door slamming shut. The sound doesn't deter me but rather has me quickening my pace, hurrying to the door.

Even with my back to him, I know he's there. I can feel him and the way he sets my body on fire. Every emotion, every desire that I have tried to ignore for God knows how many years hits me like a damn truck.

It's not until we're safely tucked away in my apartment that I find the strength to face him. And when I finally do, what I see is the last thing I ever expected.

Disheveled.

It's the only word I can think of to describe the man standing before me.

Where he is normally strong, cool, and collected – a confident man with the world at his fingertips, he now looks anything but. Emotion swirls in his brown eyes, giving me a glimpse of the boy I met over a decade ago.

"What is going on with you tonight?" I ask him.

He doesn't speak, just closes the gap between us, the look in his eyes predatory. Strong hands cup my face, tilting my head in just the right direction until our lips crash together.

The kiss is hard and demanding. His lips beg for more while mine hesitate out of mere shock. It doesn't deter him; I'm not sure anything could. He just continues to assault my lips and my senses as his tongue slips between my stunned parted lips.

When he pulls back, breaking the spell that he had me under, I just stand there staring at him. Eyes wide, heart open, I stare and search for some sign as to where in the hell this is coming from.

The desire I see in his eyes, it's for me. Not for some random woman, and knowing that ignites something inside me. I no longer care where it's coming from or how we got here. All I know is that whatever it is, I don't want it to stop.

I want this.

I want him.

So much that I take a leap I never thought that I would.

I kiss him. My hands sliding behind his head as I thread my fingers through his hair. I give myself to him – body and soul – despite the fact that my brain is having a hard time trying to conceptualize what is happening.

The moment I feel his fingers grip my ass, digging into my flesh, any residual thoughts not associated with how fucking good he feels escape me. I'm lost. In a haze. And I never want to be found.

There is swift precision in the way he moves. Every touch, every kiss filled with knowledge, skill – something he seems to have in spades, whether it be on the field or in the bedroom.

He has me pressed against the wall, his body pinning me as his hands move the skirt of my dress around my waist. Fingers dip between my parted thighs, the ones wrapped tightly around his waist. There's a sharp inhale when those fingers meet wet, smooth skin rather than the material I am sure he expected to find there.

He pulls back, his sex soaked fingers brushing over my lip. My tongue darts out, licking the arousal that he stirred in me off of them.

"Fuck." It's not a curse but a growl.

Mason Ford is not a patient man. Every ounce of restraint that he is exhibiting at this moment comes undone. I undo the top of my dress, my breasts spilling out of the top. I'm a sex crazed mess pressed against the wall, and I don't even care. Between the lust, the desperate and chaotic kisses, I can hear the buckle of his belt. The zipper. The material falling to the floor.

His head drops to my shoulder as he presses into me without abandon. There's nothing gentle, nothing sweet, pure lust driving our need. I cry out, the pleasure and pain from the unexpected thrilling me and sending something resembling electricity coursing through me. He doesn't apologize, doesn't ask if I'm okay, or even allow me a moment to adjust. He just pulls back out and thrusts right back in.

With him imbedded deep inside me, reaching places that I never even knew existed before, his lips find mine again. Hands exploring my body, areas that he had never before seen, let alone touched. The feeling of his thumb brushing over my nipple sends me over the edge. I buck against him, my clit grinding against his stomach, providing the extra pressure that I need to send me spiraling. Undoing me.

This is Mason.

This is us.

My fingers dig into the skin on his back as my orgasm rolls over me, his name escaping me and coming out as a strangled cry.

Wanting to please him the way he just set my world on fire, I moan out the word, "Couch."

With my legs still wrapped around him, he maneuvers us toward the couch. "Sit."

I'm seated on his lap, his cock settled near my entrance. A twitch of desire, a twitch of need. Raising my hips, I reach between us, taking ahold of him and settling his hardness right inside my opening – just a tease, just the tip. He wants more. I can sense it, feel it. When his lips wrap around my nipple, sucking it hard, I slam down on him.

"Oh fuck," he cries out, his head falling back on the couch.

He laces his fingers behind his head, his eyes taking in the view before him. His cock buried in me, my hands in my hair, my tits bouncing as I ride him with reckless abandon.

Years of pent-up desire take hold, and the moment his thumb presses against my clit, I fall over the edge. I spiral, free falling into orgasmic bliss. And just when I think I can't handle anymore, he grabs my hips and quickens the pace, each thrust harder, faster, and deeper.

He calls out my name, pressing me down on him one last time before pulling back out and finishing on me, his cum splattering my body as though he's marking me, branding me, possessing me.

My hand rests on his expanding chest, while he takes deep breaths trying to suck in air. We remain like this for a moment, more out of my sheer terror and inability to wrap my head around what just happened and where in the hell we go from here. An awkwardness surfaces, and I panic. I scoot back from him, the evidence of what we just did running down my body as I bolt for the bathroom.

Once inside, I rest against the door and try to catch my breath. And my mind. It seems that I managed to lose both of them the minute Mason kissed me.

He did more than kiss me. We did more than kiss. Oh, my God, what did we do?

I sink to the floor, tears stinging my eyes. What only moments ago seemed like a dream come true now seems like a disaster.

Mason is my best friend. Even more, he's my family. The only one I have. I can't lose him. And allowing this to happen, I put all of that at risk.

My hand rests against my chest, my heart aching because I know that I may have just destroyed the best thing that ever happened to me while at the same time being a dream come true. Because, if I'm honest, I have wanted this moment for so long. I have wanted him for so long. There is no other man in the world who has ever come close to making me feel the way Mason does.

While I know all of that rings true for me, I'm certain it doesn't for him.

We need to talk about this. We need to figure out what happened and where we go from here. We've known each other most of our lives. We can do this.

My hand trembles as I reach for the doorknob. I take a deep breath and exhale, then repeat the process again before pulling the door open and stepping into the living room.

"Mason, we…" I begin to say.

My eyes glance around the empty room. He's gone. In fact, it's like he was never even here.

Chapter 8

Mason

I pace around the living room, waiting for Hunter to say something.

Anything.

After racing out of Avery's apartment, I headed straight home. My mind wouldn't stop racing no matter what I did. I paced. I drank. Then, I paced some more. The whole while, all I could think about was Avery and I having sex. And how much I wanted to do it again.

I needed help. I needed someone to talk to, so I called Hunter, begged him to come over.

The moment he stepped foot inside, I bombarded him with the night's events. The jealousy I felt. Taking Avery home. The sex.

Not the details, just that it happened. The details are only for me. The taste of her kiss, the way she felt when I slid into her, the way she moved her body. All things that are now permanently ingrained in my mind.

"About damn time," he says cheerfully, despite the yawn that follows. "I'm happy for you, man."

I am sure he is. I'm sure he thinks that I've come to my senses, realized that he and Quinn are right, and decided to make a play for Avery.

When I don't say anything, the expression on his face falls. He doesn't even need to ask to know it's bad. "God damn it, Mason."

He's disappointed in me. I know because I am too.

He's more than wide awake now. His eyes are on me, studying me as if he's trying to figure out what in the hell is wrong with me.

It's a good question.

I've been asking myself the same thing since I left Avery.

Why in the hell did I have sex with Avery?

Why did I fuck her?

Let her fuck me?

What in the hell was that anyway? She felt so damn good and moved even better. If I close my eyes tight enough, I can still feel her and taste her. She was fucking perfection in every way. It blindsided me, just like when she first walked into the room in that red dress.

Ever since I walked out of her place, I've been racking my brain trying to figure out where in the hell all of this was coming from. How have I spent the past twelve years with her by my side and never noticed how gorgeous she was?

And where in the fuck did she learn to move like that?

Scratch that. That is one question I don't want to think about.

"I know, okay," I reply. "I just... she looked so good and then he had his hands on her.... and..."

"And what?"

"Fuck." I shout out the expletive because I don't have the answer he's looking for. Nothing beyond saying I'm an asshole and that he can't have her. When I don't answer, he just stares at me. Waiting. His eyes telling me I need to answer, and I need to answer him now. "She's mine. He can't have her."

"Yours?" The smile returns to Hunter's face. It screams, "I told you so, asshole."

But he's wrong. He and Quinn both are because they think this was some sort of unrequited love when all we did was have sex. Great sex, but sex nonetheless. Sex and jealousy. Jealous that she was with him. Jealous that he was trying to take what's mine. I'm fucking confused as hell why I kept thinking of her as mine. Why I still do.

My Avery.

Sexy as hell Avery. The woman that smelled like vanilla and tasted even better. The woman who is so much more than just some flimsy hook up from a bar. No. Avery instilled so much more in me. Things that I don't know what to make of or how to process. Things that made me bolt the minute she left the room.

Sex. Emotion. Need. Want.

Revenge.

I needed to claim her. Show Trent exactly who Avery belongs to.

Avery is my savior. My everything. The only person in my life with the ability to pull me from the dark and make everything better. No matter how bad things got or how much worse they became, the minute I am with her, it all goes away. Always has. Just not like she did tonight.

"Yes, mine, okay? Happy now?" I shout. "And there was no way in hell I was going to let him have her. He's taking enough from me; he can't have her, too."

"Wait, what?" Hunter looks flabbergasted by my words and a whole lot more pissed than he was at me just moments ago. "So, you're telling me that you did this to get back at him because you think he's gunning for your position on the team? This had nothing to do with Avery or you having feelings for her? This was all just to what, prove a point to Trent?"

"What do you want me to say, Hunt? I fucked her to prove she's mine and that I won't let him take what's mine? Not my spot on the team, and sure as hell, not Avery. Fine, I said it. She's mine, and I won't let him have her."

"Won't let him have me?" Her voice breaks through the rage circulating in my head. It calms every damn nerve inside my body except the ones currently filling with fear at the idea that I may have just done irreparable damage to our friendship. If I hadn't already.

"Avery," I say her name, utterly shocked by her presence. There's a horrified look on her face. One that I can't bear knowing I put there. "I didn't mean that how it sounds."

"No? So, you didn't fuck me just to get back at Trent for trying to take your spot on the team?"

I stand there silently, unable to disagree with her. It's more than that, but yeah, that was a part of it.

My lack of response allows her to continue on and give me the berating that I deserve. "You used me, Mason. You used me to get back at some guy for playing the field as good as you?"

"No, it's not like that. I just..."

"Just, what?" she shouts at me, tears streaming down her face. There's a heaviness in my chest. An ache so deep, so unlike anything I've ever felt before. And I've done some pretty dickish things in my life. Never to her though. Never to Avery. "You know what? Forget it. I don't even care."

"Avery…" Her name falls from my lips as an apology, an explanation – whatever the hell she needs it to be so long as she doesn't walk away. That's exactly what she's doing, though, isn't it?

I run my hand through my hair as I watch her walk out the door and, more than likely, out of my life.

"Go after her, you idiot," Hunter orders me.

Should I though? After this, after what I did to her, maybe she's better off without me.

I already knew that she deserved better. Better than me. Better than Trent. Better than anyone on this damn planet. So maybe, this is for the best.

"Are you seriously going to throw away the only person in this world that you love?" Hunter asks. "Because if you let her walk out that door. If you don't try? You'll lose her forever. Is that what you want?"

Fuck no, it isn't what I want. But what I want and what's best for her don't necessarily coincide. Hunter's right, though. I can't lose her. Not like this. Not because of sex. Not because apparently, I'm even more like him than I realized.

I charge out of my condo, the elevator door closing just as I reach it. My hand slams against the metal as my feet move to head for the stairs. Ten flights. That's all I have to make. I take two steps at a time, my feet pounding the tile, hurrying to catch the one thing I'm certain now that I can't lose.

"Avery, wait, please," I say when I catch her outside. My hand is on her arm, stopping her. She yanks it out of my hold as she looks at me with complete disdain, tears streaming down her face.

"Don't touch me. Don't think about me. Don't even say my name," she orders me. "How could you do that to me? How could you let me make a fool out of myself? All so you could tell Trent that you won?"

"You don't understand."

"I understand plenty," she shouts at me. "I understand that you played me. You used me, and then you were done with me."

"I am far from done with you," I argue with her, my voice filled with anger at her assumption. I may not fully understand what I'm saying, or hell, even what I'm feeling in this moment, but I know I can't lose her. I know my life is shit without her by my side.

"Yeah, well, I'm done with you. I was supposed to be different. We were supposed to be different. All you did was turn me into just another play in your playbook." She turns on her heel and begins to walk.

"Do not, walk away from me." The words come out as an order, harsh and demanding as if I have sort of control over her.

Her head whips back toward me. "Who the hell even are you right now?"

Apparently, I'm the guy that makes bad situations worse. "I'm sorry, okay. I just… I don't understand what's happening or what I'm feeling. All I know is that I can't lose you."

"Too late for that."

"Please, come back inside so we can talk."

"You've said enough for both of us." She turns and begins to walk down the street – away from me.

This time, I don't stop her. How can I? Why should I? I deserve every bit of her anger. I should suffer for every ounce of hurt I caused her. If for no other reason than the fact that I was supposed to be the one person that didn't cause her pain. I was supposed to protect her from it.

I walk back into my condo, Hunter's eyes meeting mine, searching them for answers. One answer. The one that tells him I fixed things.

"She's gone," I say somberly.

His face falls. "I'm sure it's not for good. She'll calm down. You guys will talk…"

I shake my head. There's no coming back for this. "No. She's gone. It's best if I just let her go."

He looks at me like I've lost my mind. Maybe I have. Or maybe, for the first time, I'm actually doing the right thing, putting someone else's needs before my own. Sure, watching Avery walk away from me hurt like hell. Something deep inside of me told me it was the right thing though. For her, at least. She deserves better than anything I can offer her. Even as a friend, apparently.

This is for the best.

Avery is better off without me.

Chapter 9

Avery

Several hours have passed since I left Mason's apartment, yet the pain hasn't dulled a bit. I wandered aimlessly around town, trying to come to terms with everything that happened. How quickly my world got turned upside down. No amount of walking. No amount of hiding in the bushes was going to make this go away.

My face is stained with tears and red with anger as I make my way into the apartment I share with Quinn and Claire. Quinn's sitting on the couch, her textbook open in her lap. The moment her eyes fall on me, she slams it shut. "Avery, honey? You okay?"

I can hear her, I can see her, but my ability to respond is gone. There are no words.

I don't know how I could have been so stupid. Or even what I thought us having sex was going to mean. He's been more than open about his distaste of relationships and love. I just thought if he were going to be with me, like that, it had to be something more, didn't it? It had to mean something. The man I know, he wouldn't hurt me. He wouldn't use me.

Except, he did.

Shutting the door behind me wasn't going to deter Quinn. I knew that the moment I did it. Still, it gave me a moment. A second to gather my bearings and decide what and how much I want to tell her.

In true Quinn fashion, she barges in without knocking. "What happened?"

"Mason. He…" I stop, unable to say the words. To admit out loud that Mason used me – that I let him – would make this all that much more real.

Through the tears, I can see the panic register on her face. My hysterics mixed with the mention of her brother, and I can only guess that she's assuming the worst.

"He's fine," I mutter. "He's an asshole, but he's fine."

Her shoulders slump in relief. She blows out a breath and rests her hands on her hips. "What did he do?"

What didn't he do is more like it? I knew this wasn't going to be the beginning of some grand romance. Sure, I hoped. But I knew that if we were going to go that route that it would take time. I'm not a fool. To hear him say that he used me to stick it to Trent? That I never expected.

I take a deep breath, inhaling all the oxygen that Mason depleted me of with his words, and exhale. "Mason and I had sex."

"You what?" Quinn exclaims. "How? When?"

"It doesn't matter. None of it matters." The tears begin to dry, anger taking its place. "He only had sex with me so Trent couldn't. To make me off-limits to Trent. To… claim me."

Quinn's face looks like I imagine mine did when I heard the words fall from his lips. "He told you this?"

"No, of course not." As if Mason would have the balls to just tell me the truth. "He said it to Hunter, and I overheard."

"I'll kill him," Quinn says as she heads for the door.

"Don't please. Just… leave it."

She stops and turns back to me. "He owes you an apology. He owes you a hell of a lot more than that, but at least it will be a start."

"He already apologized," I tell her. "Let's face it though, we both know that he only apologized because he got caught. What he said, Q, it's the truth. It doesn't matter if I know it or not. It is a fact. One that I can't live with."

Her arms wrap around me, pulling me into a hug. I hold her tightly. The only person who normally can comfort me is the one person I need comfort from. How's that for a kick in the ass?

"You know he loves you. You mean everything to him."

Maybe I do. Maybe I don't. But the ache in my heart makes me not care.

"I keep telling myself I shouldn't be surprised. This is Mason after all. I just... I never thought I would be the field he'd want to play on. And I sure as hell never thought he would do it just to get back at Trent."

"I'm sure there's more to it than that. You know Mason...."

"That's just it. I thought I did. But now? I'm not so sure."

"Something isn't right. Mason would never do anything to intentionally hurt you," Quinn says in defense of her brother.

A defense that I fully understand her making but don't want to hear right now.

"He didn't, Quinn. He didn't hurt me intentionally because he didn't intend on me hearing the truth," I reply.

"Had I not walked in when I did, he would have just continued to make a fool out of me."

"Avery…" Quinn says.

"No. I'm sorry, Quinn, I don't want to hear it. I don't want any excuses. I just… he was the one person I trusted, and he used me. And for what? Sex? Do I really mean that little to him that he would do this?"

I sink to the floor, the ache in my chest unbearable. Quinn's arms are around me, comforting me. She doesn't speak; she just holds me.

"I think it's because you mean that much to him," Quinn replies. "And I don't think he knows how to handle it." Before I can plead with her to quit defending him, she apologizes. "I'm sorry, Ave. I'm sorry for what my idiot brother did. I'm sorry for making excuses for him. I'm sorry that he's a damn fool and doesn't realize how amazing the two of you would be together."

"Thanks."

"Why don't we go out? Grab some dinner? Some drinks?"

"Did I hear someone say drinks?" Claire says, popping her head into the room. Her face falls the minute she sees my tear stained one. "What's going on?"

Claire is one of the kindest souls I've met. She just has this almost maternal feel to her. The ultimate caregiver. So, the minute she puts her arms around me. I crumble. Again.

I sit there, wondering if I'm ever going to be able to put the pieces back together.

Quinn does me a favor of filling in Claire, so I don't have to recount each and every gory detail – again.

"Holy Toledo." It's all Claire says, and frankly, I'm right there with her.

What else can I say? Or do? It's just… wow.

"You seriously need drinks. I call girls night."

"Yes, girls' night," Quinn agrees.

I shake my head as I wipe the tears away. "I can't. I'm not in the mood to go out."

Claire stands proudly. "Then we'll bring the booze to you."

Quinn's phone begins to ring in her pocket, the ringtone a familiar tune that I know means Hunter is on the other end.

"Answer it," I tell her.

She rests her head on my shoulder. "He can wait."

"I appreciate it, but I just want to be alone. I need to process," I say.

The ringing dies down but picks right back up again.

"The last thing you need is to be alone," Claire says. "What you need to do is drink."

"And vent," Quinn chimes in. "Just please don't tell me what my brother is like in bed."

The gagging sounds she is making cause me to crack a smile.

"Oh God, it's too late. I'm already picturing it," she continues. "My eyes!"

I'm full blown laughing now, Claire joining in.

"Why do you even care, anyway?" Claire asks. "There a million football players out there."

"Like Trent," Quinn says.

"Or Billy. Billy is so hot," Claire says as she fans herself.

I fall back on the bed. "Honestly…"

"If you even tell me he ruined you for other men, I am so throwing up all over your comforter." There's a smirk on Quinn's face.

"I don't ever want to… anything… another football player again."

Claire lies next to me, her platinum blonde head pressing against mine. "Thank God. Time to move on to a real sport. Shall we start scouting some baseball players?"

"Better yet… hockey." Quinn's smirk turns more devilish as she speaks.

"Don't let Hunter hear you say that," I tease.

"Please. That man has most definitely ruined me for other men," she says, forming her hands into a rather large O.

My hand flies over my eyes, trying not to catch a glimpse of her hand gesture. The conversation has turned so ridiculous at this point that I can't help but laugh. Really laugh.

At least until I hear the sound of my phone and the familiar ring tone it's playing.

Both girls look at me. "Don't answer."

"I wasn't planning on it," I say, sitting up straight. "I told him we're done. And I mean it." I shove off the bed and head toward the kitchen. "Where's that alcohol you both were promising?"

As I pour the tequila into the shot glass, memories of my one perfect moment with Mason flood me. The kisses, the touches, the screaming each other's names in sheer pleasure. It's as though I can still feel him every touch, every kiss. I close my eyes, trying to hold onto it, trying to unhear the words I heard him say to Hunter.

I slam the shot and then another. The alcohol not soothing the ache like it's supposed to. Quinn and Claire join me, each of them trying their damnedest to cheer me up. I don't want to be cheered up though. I can't be. Not yet, at least.

I need to mourn. I need to grieve.

When I finally return to my room, I slide into bed and pull the blankets high up around me. I'm hoping the drunken state I put myself in helps sleep come easier, but I make the mistake of glancing at my phone first.

Five missed calls. Twenty missed texts. Like a fool, I listen to and read every message.

Mason: Avery, I am so sorry. Please let me explain.

Mason: I know how it sounded, but I didn't mean it like that.

Mason: Please answer so I can explain.

Mason: You have to know that I never meant to hurt you.

Mason: You know how much you mean to me.

Mason: I'm so sorry. I will make it up to you. Somehow.

Mason: Please, Avery. Hear me out.

With the phone in my hand and tears in my eyes, the ringing begins again.

I connect the call but don't give him the opportunity to speak. I'm drunk and exhausted, and I just can't do this anymore. "Just leave me alone, Mason."

His voice is soft, "I can't do that. Not until you hear me out. I didn't mean it. I wouldn't use you. Fuck, Ave, you know that the last thing in the world I ever want to do is hurt you."

"It's a little late for that."

"I know. I'm sorry, Avery."

"So am I."

"Let me fix this. I can fix it. I just need to explain. Trent got in my head. And then you wore that dress. And…"

"Stop. Please, just stop." Sadness overcomes me, the sob I had been trying to hold back emerging in the form of a strangled cry.

"I can't. I can't lose you."

I try to breathe, to suck in the air that I seem to be lacking. "You… you already did," I tell him as I disconnect the phone and turn it off.

Mason is nothing if not persistent. I just can't take anymore tonight.

The ache in my heart isn't entirely his fault. The pain is real though. Unbearable. And there's nothing he can say to change what we did or what we've become.

Chapter 10

Mason

Absolute shit.

That's what life has been since Avery walked out of my life. I practice for shit. I look like shit. No signs of anything changing anytime soon either because there's no going back. When I let her walk away from me, I knew it was for the best.

It's killing me inside, but it's definitely for the best.

For the first time since Coach told me Trent was going to be starting, he sacked me. I was distracted, just like I have been all week. Only today, my anger has subsided, and misery has taken over. He took me down, and I didn't even fucking care.

On the plus side, my lack of caring took the enjoyment right out of it for him.

As I stalk into the locker room, I berate myself again for having hurt the person that I care about the most. I lost Avery, and if I keep going like this, I'm going to lose my spot on the team, too. And I only have myself to blame. I can't even blame the shit on dickhead Trent even if I wanted to. No, this is all on me. And if I fuck this up, I'll be left with nothing.

No Avery.

No team.

Nothing.

I can't help it though. No matter what I do, I can't seem to pull myself out of this funk. This whole thing with Avery has me fucked in the head. Two weeks have passed since we slept together. Since she walked out of my life – most likely for good. Both instances affecting my head and my heart.

"Any luck with Avery?" Hunter asks.

Part of me wishes there were and part of me truly believes that she's better off without me in her life. "I already told you, I got what I deserved. I'm not going to push her."

Though, that's exactly what I did the night everything went to hell. I bombarded her with text messages. Then phone calls. Until she finally answered. I regretted calling her the moment that I heard her anguished voice begging me to leave her alone.

That's when it hit me. That's when I realized what I did, how badly I destroyed our friendship. I gave her my sincerest apology, deep and heartfelt. She could hear it in my voice, I'm sure. But apology or not, this isn't getting fixed.

"You're just going to give up?" he presses.

"Back off, Hunt."

"No. I am not going to let you do this. You made a mistake. Mistakes can be fixed."

"Not this one." I punch the metal of the locker. "I hurt her, Hunt. I was supposed to be the one to protect her, and yet, here I am – the one that hurt her."

"Don't worry, Adams. I'll kiss it and make it better for you." I hear Trent's voice behind me.

"You son-of-a-bitch," I shout, turning in his direction. My feet move, my body charging toward his, "You stay the fuck away from her."

Hunter's hands are on me, holding me back.

"Didn't sound like that's what she wanted when she called me last night," Trent says, a smug smirk plastered on his stupid face.

Unsure of whether or not he's just trying to goad me, I continue on my tirade. "If you lay a hand on her," I shout, breaking free from Hunter's hold, rage filling me and taking over. My hands fist his shirt as I slam him against the wall. "I will..."

"Knock it off," Coach shouts. There's a look of disappointment on his face. One that is directed solely at me.

"Walk away, Mase," Hunter urges me.

"She belongs to me, asshole. So does this team," I state as I grab my bag and throw it over my shoulder before storming out of the locker room and straight to the closest damn bar.

Pulling my hat down to cover my face, I'm grateful the hole in the wall bar I stumbled across isn't too crowded. I slide into the barstool tucked in the corner, hoping no one but the bartender notices me.

There's a burly old man tending bar. He makes his way to me and smiles. "What can I get you, son?"

Son? The only one who's ever called me that was Coach Reed. My parents preferred to use terms of endearment like asshole or shithead. Hearing this guy call me son stirs up a shit ton of emotion that I don't think I can quite handle on top of everything else.

"Tequila. And keep it coming," I say, sliding a hundred-dollar bill across the bar as I do.

The bartender eyes the money, then looks back at me. "You okay?"

"Not even close," I reply.

"You want to talk about it?" he asks as he grabs the bottle of tequila from the shelf behind him.

I look up at him from under the bill of my hat. "I want to drink about it."

"Then drink away," he says, setting the bottle in front of me. "Just make sure you don't try to drive."

I give him a nod before taking my first drink.

Drink after drink, I sit here in the corner trying to rid my mind of Avery. It's an impossible feat. Her, Hunter, and Quinn, they are all that I have. That's it. They're my family – my everything.

So why in the fuck did I risk it? Why would I risk her? Us? Our friendship?

Just because my dick got hard at the sight of her? Because she looked so damn good?

Her, in that dress, it's what sucked me in. The taste of her, the feel of her, it's what made me insatiable. Christ, she felt amazing. And the way she moved was like an angel sent straight from hell.

There was more to it, though. For the first time ever, sex was more than just sex. More than pleasure. She made me feel. Her gorgeous eyes pulling me in and making me want things that I can't have. The very things I can't give her.

It's why I left. Because I couldn't handle the feelings, or rather, how she made me feel.

Correction, how she makes me feel.

Because nothing has changed since that day. The emotions are still present. I don't know why they surfaced, nor do I understand them, but they're there all the same.

And now she's gone.

Avery. The one person who helps me figure shit out, shows me how to navigate feelings that are so fucking foreign to me. Without her, I don't know what to do, how to function. And I don't want to learn. I just want her back.

For the past twelve years, we were inseparable. One night. That's all it took to tear us apart.

Get off your ass, Mason, and fix shit with Avery.

I fight the urge to follow the direction that my subconscious is steering me in. I try to remind myself that Avery is better off without me.

But you're not better off without her.

Emotion wells up in me, and I swallow the lump that forms in my throat. The sentiment may be selfish, but it's true. I am nothing without her.

Go to her. Go to her right now and fix it. Do whatever it takes.

Drunk off my ass; I put more money on the bar and slide off the barstool.

"Hey, kid, this is too much," the bartender says.

I give him a weak smile. "Well deserved."

With that, I stumble out the door and to the curb where the Uber I called is waiting.

"Holy shit, you're Mason Ford," the driver says when I climb into the backseat.

"Yay," I say sarcastically.

"You're my favorite player, hands down. I have like five of your jerseys…."

"Why?" I ask him. Curiosity and my drunken stupor getting the best of me.

"Why not? You're amazing on the field and off. The charity work you do, the coaching at the university. You're amazing."

"Yeah, I'm a real prince," I say sarcastically.

"The people you help think you are. I know. A friend of mine actually benefited from your football scholarship program. Dude was headed toward a dark path, but that… that saved him."

I hate the smile hearing that brings to my face. I hate that it makes me feel even slightly better about myself when I've spent the better part of two weeks telling myself what an asshole I am. I don't deserve to feel good. But his words make me think that maybe I'm not a complete asshole after all.

"Thanks, man. I needed that."

"Where to?"

"Remington University Apartments," I say. "Building C."

"Hot date?"

I chuckle. "Nah. Just trying to fix something I messed up."

It's a short drive to the campus apartments but listening to Tad talk about how much he adores me sobers me some. For a moment, I even second guess the low opinion I currently have of myself and question whether or not I'm really like my dad.

"Thanks, man," I say when the car pulls up in front of the building. He really seems like a genuine fan, not some douche who's going to post pics of the drunk defensive end all over the internet. I pull out what's left of the cash in my wallet and hand it to him. He begins to argue but notices the business card on the top.

"What's this?" he asks.

"Shoot me an email with your info," I say. "Would love to have my biggest fan at one of the home games."

"You're the best. Thanks."

I shut the door behind me and, still drunk, I stagger inside the building. Let's hope that I can live up to good old Tad's high opinion of me.

I stare at the elevator, the out-of-order sign staring back at me. Just my damn luck that the elevator's out. On unsteady feet, I make the trek up the three flights of stairs. I'm a little winded and a whole lot tired when I reach the top. My fist connects with the wooden door, the emotions surging through me taking over. So much for the guy that Tad thought I was. Here I am pounding on the door, begging and pleading for her to open it. There is movement on the other side, yet the door remains unanswered.

"Open the door, Avery," I shout as I continue to bang my hand against the door to her apartment.

This continues for ten minutes. Ten minutes of nonstop knocking. Ten minutes of pure agony. Ten minutes of living in despair. Numerous people have stuck their heads out of their doors, looking to see what the commotion is. I don't give a damn about any of them. All I care about is getting Avery to answer the door.

Frustrated and angry, I yell, "Open the fucking door."

The emotion pouring out of me is exhausting. I've kept anything even close to resembling emotions at bay for most of my life. I don't let them in, and I sure as hell don't let them out. Until now. I rest my forehead against the door, and when I do, it opens slightly.

"Go away, Mason," Claire tells me.

"I just want to talk to her," I plead. I'm scared and desperate. And, drunk. So, fucking drunk.

"Well, she doesn't want to talk to you. And you standing out here causing a drunken scene isn't going to change that."

I know that Claire is right. No amount of pounding on the door or begging and pleading is going to fix what I've done. Nothing is going to make Avery forgive me. I have to try though, don't I? At least make her see that I am sorry, that I never meant to hurt her. I can't just give up on her. Or on us.

"Tell her that I'm sorry. Tell her I didn't mean it."

Just then, Avery pushes past Claire. "Didn't mean it? Bullshit, Mason." She's shouting loud enough to re-disturb all the neighbors that had just retreated to their apartments. "So, then you didn't use me? You didn't take me home with the intention of fucking me just to prove to Trent that you could? That you won whatever little pissing match the two of you are in? Or is that just how you treat all your one-night stands?"

She stands there with her hands on her hips, staring me down.

"You're…" I shake my head, hating the way the words sound and hating even more that she's using them in reference to herself. "You are not a one-night stand."

"Well, it sure as hell isn't happening again. Your behavior pretty much screamed how little our friendship means to you."

"No, that's… you're wrong. Our friendship…it…"

"Was a mistake?" she supplies.

"No. Never." I hang my head. "Fuck, Ave, come on. You know me better than that."

"I thought I did."

With my head hung, I plead with her, "Please, just let me in so I can explain."

"I let you in once. And look where that got me."

"That's not fair."

"I don't give a damn what you think is fair or not. I just want you to stay out of my life."

The door slams in my face.

My head hangs, my heart broken, and I realize it's over.

I lost Avery.

Chapter 11

Avery

Setting my caramel macchiato down on the table, I give Quinn a soft apologetic smile as she rants and raves about Mason's most recent behavior.

One month. One long month since the day I left the club with Mason. Since we had sex and, in turn, threw away everything that we spent twelve years building. One month since nothing in my entire world has looked, or felt, right.

Everything feels off. And from what Quinn's been telling me, along with what I've seen on social media, Mason's feeling it, too. He's drinking and partying more than he ever has before. He has the Red Devils organization in such a tailspin that he's losing playing time.

"Can you believe that?" she asks, recounting to me several of the self-destructive moves that he's made.

The truth is, I can.

Mason and me, we were more than just friends. We were a support system of sorts, balancing each other out and keeping our lives on an even keel. Without the other around, it's a little harder to navigate this thing we call life. So, the fact that he's acting out, drinking incessantly, it doesn't surprise me. I would probably be doing the same thing if I didn't have Quinn and Claire to ground me, to force me out of my depression and back into life.

The part that doesn't make any sense to me is him throwing his career away. The more he acts out, the more play time the team gives Trent. And much to all of our dismay, Trent's killing it on the field. He's no Mason, no one is, but when you add in Mason's bad attitude and reckless behavior, Trent looks like a much more viable option.

He, however, is not an option for me. Trent has continued to call me to try and coerce me into going on a date with him. When once the idea of sticking it to Mason seemed appealing, it sure as hell doesn't now. Not since I realized I was just a pawn at the center of some pissing match between the two of them.

"I'm sorry, I shouldn't be telling you this stuff. You don't need to hear it after what he did to you," she apologizes.

"I appreciate that, but I'm still your friend. And clearly, you're upset." I rest my hand on hers. "You can talk to me about anything, Q, even Mason."

"No, what I should be doing is asking how you are. Are you okay?"

I take a sip of the caramel macchiato as I contemplate my answer.

Am I okay?

The easy answer would be yes, I'm fine. And to a degree, I am. I go about my day-to-day life, school, work, all of it, without issue. The days are busy and filled with things to occupy my mind. It's when the day turns into night that the sadness begins to settle in. The sadness and the memories. Lately, those memories have been turning into nightmares that I thought I had rid myself of years ago. But it seems there was a driving force behind those nightmares disappearing, a person who calmed the storm inside me enough to ease me to sleep. That person, he's no longer here to do that.

Just like I'm not there to do it for him.

I would be lying if I said that I hadn't reached for my phone to call him on more the one occasion. I have. He's the only one that knows about the nightmares, the truth behind them. Pieces of my past that come flooding back to me. Pieces that I don't want to share with anyone else.

They're our secrets. Only ours.

I just wish that all of this meant as much to him as it does to me. Did to me, I correct myself. Though, I know it's untrue. My feelings for Mason, they haven't dulled or changed the way that I had hoped they would. If anything, they've only grown with a rapid intensity. Every piece of me dying to reach out to him because somewhere beyond my anger and hurt, I know that I matter to him. I know that all of this is hurting him just as much as it is me. While I might want to reach out, might want to forgive and forget, I can't.

That doesn't lie solely with him. It's me too.

We were friends.

Best friends.

And I made the mistake of falling for him.

And now I can't take back what we did or erase the memory of it. I can't set things back to where they were before my heart betrayed me and gave itself to him without permission. As angry as I am, as hurt as I feel, I know that trying to rekindle any part of us will only result in me being hurt further. No matter how much I love him, he will never love me back. And I can't go on like that anymore. I can't pretend anymore. Not now.

"I'm fine, Quinn," I say. "Really."

She nods her head, but she knows I'm lying.

"So, what's going on with Mason?" I ask, even though I already know.

He's a high-profile guy. His handsome face plastered over more tabloids than any movie star or royalty, especially as of late. His most recent tragic event, a one car accident involving him and a tree, made front page news. Luckily, he wasn't hurt. Still, the press is having a field day with it. With him.

The downfall of a football great.

He's out of control, and for the life of me, I can't figure out what made him spiral this far out of control.

Maybe things with Trent have worsened. Maybe the organization is pushing harder at moving Mason out. Whatever it is, it's pushed him over the edge.

The same way feeling his lips on mine did to me. So enamored with him, so in love, I allowed myself to be blinded to the reality of the situation and instead allowed myself to just live in the moment. To take that moment and run with it knowing it would be my only chance. What I never thought of, what I never even considered, was that it would break us.

I didn't think anything could.

Whatever it is that's going on with him, it's eating him alive.

Quinn hesitates for a moment before speaking. "Please don't take this the wrong way, but all I can think is that it has something to do with you."

I shake my head, unwilling to be his excuse. "No."

"I'm not blaming you..."

"I would hope not. This has nothing to do with me. It's because of Trent and the team and him being afraid that it's being taken from him. That's what's doing this. That's what sent him into this tailspin."

"Maybe. And maybe that's also what spiraled him into your arms that night, but that is not what has sent him this far over the edge." Quinn sighs as she leans back in her seat. "You know as well as I do that nothing can break Mason. Except maybe you."

I cock my head to the side. "Did he put you up to this? Is this some sort of ambush?"

"No. Of course not. Nothing like that. This is all me. I just... I hate this. I feel like a kid with divorced parents, stuck in the middle between two of the most important people in my life. I just... I miss my family, and I just want us all back together again. Isn't there any way to fix this?"

Hell bent on being angry and keeping my distance, if for no other reason than keeping my heart from breaking further, I shake my head. "No." I sigh. "I wish there were. But... after how we grew up, the things we went through... I swore to myself that I would never let anyone use me, or abuse me, or... well, hurt me ever again." Mason had promised that too – he would never let anyone hurt me.

Including myself. Pursuing even a friendship with Mason at this point, it's not going to do anything except cause me more heartbreak. I thought I could handle it, but

I can't. It's best to break ties now, move on, and maybe even find my happy ending.

Maybe.

"I know." She gives my hand a comforting squeeze.

"Whatever he's doing, whatever he's getting himself into – just be there for him. He needs someone. And he doesn't trust anyone except you and Hunter."

"And you," she reminds me.

"But I can't be there for him. Not anymore."

One slip up. One night of passion. And we are done.

He did exactly what he set out to do – he claimed me. He made me his in every way possible. Including the very ways that he can never be mine.

"I understand."

I know that she isn't just saying it either. She knows how hard this is for me because she knows exactly how much Mason means to me. She understands that Mason hurt me and that I can't forgive him for that. She also understands that I can't because having been with him now, having taken that leap, my heart can't handle it. I fell right over the edge and into a place where Mason became more than a friend. Maybe it was inevitable. Maybe I was fooling myself thinking that this could last when obviously it couldn't.

At some point, my heart was bound to give out. There is only so much strength one can possess when denying themselves the one thing they love. Really, what did I think would happen? How in the world was me loving him and him not reciprocating those feelings going to last?

"I almost forgot." She pulls out an envelope and extends it to me. "This came for you."

My hands tremble as I take the envelope from her. "This better not be from Mason."

"Do I look crazy to you?" she asks with a laugh. "There is no way in hell I am playing the go between. You two will work it out. Eventually."

"I'm glad you seem to have so much faith in us," I tease.

"I have to. You guys are my family. All the Christmas' we shared, just the three of us. The sleepovers in the old apartment. The way you and I would sneak alcohol in, and Mason would catch us and punish us." The smile the memories brought to her fades, her gaze dropping to her hands. "I just hate to think that we'll never all be together again."

I cock my head to the side. "Are you seriously trying to guilt trip me?"

There's a sheepish look on her face. "Is it working?"

"Not a chance," I laugh.

"Whatever. Can't blame a girl for trying," she says as she jumps to her feet.

"Why don't you go give Hunter that sob story," I tease. "Maybe he'll kiss it and make it all better."

"Oh, he will. And I don't need any sob story to get him to do it." She taps her finger against her chin. "What about you? Would that work for you?"

"Would what work for me?"

"Having someone kiss it and make it better? Like, I don't know, maybe... Billy?"

"How did you…"

I think of Billy and our dinner the other night. He had made a pit stop in town to visit his family, and we just happened to run into each other. Before I knew it, we were having dinner and drinks, and I was laughing for the first time in what felt like forever.

It felt so good to feel good again that I let the alcohol get to my head, and I kissed him. Regret washed over me the minute my lips met his. Billy and Mason have always been rivals on and off the field, and the last thing I need is to get between another two men. Nope. Not happening.

Thankfully, Billy was nothing but kind. He took the kiss for what it was worth. He told me what a great friend I am and gave his sincerest apologies for the position that Mason and I are in.

Then he agreed to keep our dinner – and our kiss – to himself.

So, how in the hell does Quinn know about it?

"I have my ways," she tells me with an evil smile on her sweet face.

"I'm not ready to be kissed by anybody. Least of all, Billy."

"You're no fun," Quinn pouts playfully.

"And you're late. Get to class," I tell her.

"I'm going, I'm going."

Chapter 12

Mason

"Jesus Christ, Mason, are you trying to destroy your career? The team?" Coach shouts at me. His voice booms, reverberating off the walls of his office.

The answer is no. Not intentionally, at least.

Seeing Avery out with Billy the other night set off something inside me. Some sort of jealous rage that far surpassed even what I felt when I saw Trent with his hands on her. Maybe because Billy's a decent guy. A guy that could actually be good for Avery. And that did not sit well with me.

It took that moment to make me see the truth. To see what has been right in front of me this whole time.

My feelings for Avery far surpass the realm of friendship; hell, they surpass anything I fucking understand. It's not as though I had the best examples growing up. Lust, not love. That's what my home revolved around. The women, the drugs, the whatever the hell else my father was doing behind closed doors when he was ignoring his wife and children.

All I know was that there was no love. I was never loved, and so, I've never loved anyone in return.

How could I when I didn't even know what the fuck the word really meant?

It took me losing Avery to realize exactly what she meant to me. Sure, I knew that she meant the world to me, but I didn't realize that world meant my heart, too. Because she does, she owns it. Every beat begins and ends with her.

And I was so fucking stupid to not have seen it sooner. Out of everyone in the world, she's the only one that really knows me, really understands me. And even with all of that, she accepts me.

She might accept me, but why in the hell would she ever want someone like me as anything more?

All of this shit hit me like a damn semi all at once. Feelings, emotions, things I don't understand and normally try to keep buried kept crashing into me. Each one knocking me down more and more until I couldn't take it anymore.

As I stood there and watched her laughing with Billy, everything began hitting me at once; I knew that everything worked out for the best. She was exactly where she should be – with a guy that deserves her.

And me?

Well, it was time I faced facts.

As much as I wish I hadn't, I've turned into my dad. It was bound to happen at some point. Hell, I've been waiting for it. Then, out of the left fucking field, it happens. The apple doesn't fall far from the tree, after all. And the tree I fell from? Rotten to the damn core. Some things you just can't escape.

All the emotions sent me into a tailspin. One that resulted in me fucking up, yet again, and led to the current reaming I am getting from Coach.

This, the accident, it's the icing on the cake of the path of destruction I've been on the last several weeks. One that began the moment I realized that I wouldn't be able to win Avery back, that I had lost my friend for good. And then further went downhill when I realized exactly how much she meant to me – that Hunter and Quinn were right.

So, when he asks the question, I don't bother to respond. I deserve every single thing he's dishing out to me. With my head hung, I sit there and take it because there is no excuse, no reason for what I did. Other than I'm a complete fucking idiot.

"What the fuck is wrong with you?" He's still shouting, and I'm still taking it.

What else can I do? While hurting myself or the team isn't intentional, I can't seem to stop it either. The same way I couldn't stop myself from hurting Avery.

"You are the best of the best. And you're going to just throw it all away on… pussy and booze?"

I laugh. Him calling me the best of the best? What a fucking joke. A complete crock of shit.

He has no idea the worst of what I've done.

Sure, there was the drinking, the partying, and the accident. But the worst of it all – throwing away the best thing that ever happened to me because I couldn't keep my fucking dick in my pants.

Avery.

Now, she's the best of the best.

Me, on the other hand, I am nothing but a fucking screw up. A dead beat. A fucking asshole, a loser who doesn't deserve to breathe the same air as her.

She may not have been my downfall, but she sure as fuck is what's keeping me on that path. Not her, not specifically. She's not the one that did anything wrong. In fact, her telling me that she never wanted to see me again was the smartest thing she could have done.

For her, at least.

For me? What's even left?

I already lost Avery, and with the path that I'm on, my football career is going down the drain too. I've got nothing left to lose.

"Do you have anything to say for yourself?" Coach shouts.

I shake my head. What is there to say? I fucked up? No shit. I'll do better? Probably not.

Coach looks at Lou, my agent, who just shrugs his shoulders.

Lou has essentially given up on me. I've never been anything more than a paycheck to him. Now, I've become nothing more than a liability to his livelihood. Coach, he's a little more invested. He shouldn't be, but he is.

I'm not quite sure if Lou called Coach or Coach called Lou, but clearly, they thought the only way to get to me was by joining forces. Lou, he's the idea guy. He has come up with many genius ideas to get my stupid ass out of shit than I can even fathom. Coach, on the other hand, he's the muscle. Frankly, I don't give a shit what Lou says about anything. I should, and if I were smart, I would because he knows his shit. However, it takes Coach and that look he gives me to actually get me to do what Lou wants. It's a fucked up process, but it is what it is.

"What we need to do," Lou begins, "is repair your whole reputation. Starting with the women."

Women? What women? I haven't so much as laid a finger on a woman since Avery, let alone done anything else with one.

Still, I suppose my reputation precedes me. Regardless of what I have been up to as of late, the world still sees me as the team playboy. And, more recently, the team fuck up. The combo is detrimental. It's one thing when I'm out screwing a bunch of women. It's another when I'm doing it and crashing my car into things. That screams downward spiral. And downward spirals are not a good thing. Especially not for a highly respected organization like the Red Devils.

My laughter fills the room. Both men look at me like I'm crazy, but I'm not. The idea of repairing my reputation is preposterous.

"Can't fix what's not broken," I tell him. "Women aren't the issue."

No, women aren't the problem. I am.

They both look at me, surprised that I'm speaking at all. And probably surprised at the idea that women aren't causing me issues. The way I run through them, correction ran through them, you would think they would be.

"Then what is the problem, Mason?" Coach Reed asks. For as furious as I know he is with me, when he asks the question, his voice softens. The fatherly side in him takes over. "Is this about Trent? I told you, Mase, I'm not replacing you."

His voice sounds both trustworthy and sincere, but I don't fucking buy it. Maybe Coach isn't trying to replace me, but the organization sure as fuck is.

"I don't give a fuck about Trent." It's a lie. I do. And while Trent may have set me on the path, it's not him keeping me here.

"Then what? What is it?"

"Me. I'm damaged. Irreparable."

"Bullshit." Coach pulls up a chair and sits in front of me, his elbows resting on his knees. "Don't pull this poor, poor me routine with me." His finger is pointed directly at me. "I know where you came from, what you've had to overcome. Don't think for one minute I buy that all this is because you've suddenly reverted to the asshole you worked so hard not to be. What the fuck happened? What happened to make you throw all your hard work out the window?"

There's a gentle undertone in his voice. Coach recruited me, drafted me, and mentored me. He isn't just professionally invested. He's emotionally invested, too.

"Nothing," I deadpan.

"I don't buy it."

"I don't give a damn what you buy or what you don't. It's the truth. Nothing happened; nothing changed me. This is who I always was. I just got sick of pretending and playing the other guy."

Coach's head drops in frustration. Normally, when the chips are down, he can get through to me. Not this time. No one can.

"What do you suggest?" Coach Reed asks Lou.

Lou has a plan. I know he does. Just like I know that whatever it is, I'm not going to like it.

"We need to start with this playboy reputation. Once people see he's not out screwing every woman that walks past him, he'll begin to look a little more…"

"More what?" I ask, curious where he is going with this.

"Wholesome."

"I am far from wholesome," I laugh.

"Shut your damn mouth," Coach demands. "You don't want to tell us what the problem is so you don't get a say in shit."

"For your information, I'm not out screwing women every night," I say defensively. I wish I were, but I just can't bring myself to. Not with the memory of Avery and our night together still so fresh in my mind.

Lou doesn't care. He just continues on babbling about me and settling down and showing the world a different side of me. Blah. Blah. Blah.

"You two can make me do a lot of shit, but you can't make me fall in love with someone," I point out.

"No, but we can pay someone to pretend to love your sorry ass," Lou replies.

I look at him as though he's grown two heads. I'm not exactly sure what he's suggesting, but I hate it. Pay someone to love me?

"Like a hooker?" I ask.

Lou rolls his eyes. "Definitely not like a hooker. Someone more…."

"Wholesome?" I supply.

Lou shoots me a look but says, "Exactly."

"And just who do you plan on paying?" I ask. I at least deserve to know what or who my money is going to. "Do I get a say?"

"Fuck no, you don't. I will not have you picking out some broad based on breast size and her willingness to put out. This isn't about getting you laid, Mason; it's about saving your ass with the organization." Coach is stern with his words, and it makes me feel like a child being reprimanded by its parents. At least, what I would assume it would be like. My parents never gave enough of a damn to reprimand me. Hell, they weren't even around most of the time. All they did was disrespect me and put me down. They used my love for them, my desire to be loved by them, against me.

Just like I did to Avery.

I used her love and friendship to satisfy my selfish and stupid needs. To stake a claim on something that I can't have.

For as much as I hate everything that's happening at the moment, I have to admit that the concern I hear in Coach's voice gives me a slight twinge of happiness. It's been a while since I've heard that – from anyone, including my own sister.

"What about your friend?" Lou asks.

"Hunter? No way in hell is anyone going to buy that I am switching teams," I say with a laugh and a shake of my head. Christ, Lou is really grasping at straws here.

"Not Hunter, you ass. The girl. What's her name?" Lou asks.

"Avery?" I supply with complete and utter confusion.

Lou snaps his fingers. "Yes, her. She would be willing to do it, I'm sure. She's always got your back."

"Had," I say. Lou cocks his head to the side, confused. "She had my back. We're uh… not exactly on speaking terms."

"Jesus, Mason, you fuck her and run too?" Lou says. There's amusement in his voice, but I find his words

anything but funny. In fact, I look down at my hands –
ashamed. "Oh, come on." Lou throws his hands in the air.

"She'll do it," Coach says.

"She won't," I argue.

"Lou, give us a minute?" Coach says. Lou leaves,
and Coach steps up to me, his hands gripping the armrests
of the chair in which I am sitting. "That girl has stood by
you through everything. She's the only one in the world
that anyone would believe would actually date you and not
just fuck you. I will arrange for you to meet with her, and
you're going to fix whatever it is you fucked up."

He knows. He knows that whatever happened
between Avery and me is what set me on this destructive
path. He also knows she's the only one who can get me off
it.

"I tried. I have tried everything," I tell him.

Phone calls, texts, flowers, a goddamn car. Nothing
worked.

"Have you tried not being a dick?" he suggests as
he stands upright. His arms cross over his chest, and he
smiles.

"Funny. Really fucking funny."

Chapter 13

Avery

The phone call I received from Coach Reed took me off guard.

Seeing Mason already sitting at the conference table when I step into the room turns my world upside down. I didn't expect him to be here already. In fact, I hadn't really expected him to show at all. Whatever is going on, it must be bad.

While I'm not entirely sure what this is, I'm almost positive it has something to do with Mason's recent erratic behavior. A behavior they need my help correcting. Now, here I stand, torn between wanting to make whatever it is he's going through go away and not giving a damn because he hurt me so badly.

I keep reminding myself that Mason's a big boy. He can take care of himself. Except that what he's struggling with at the moment are emotions and those he doesn't have the slightest clue how to handle.

Mason has spent his entire life fighting to not turn into his father. The differences between the two are astounding. There is no way that Mason could ever be like his father; still, he fears it. It's that fear that drives everything he does. His lack of emotional connection, his drive for perfection on the field. He is always rallying around Quinn and me, telling us that we could do better than the lives we were dealt when it seems like he doesn't find that to be true for himself. He doesn't see how it already is. How it could be so much better.

He may have made a hell of a life for himself as a professional football player, but he sure as hell hasn't in any other aspect. There was one moment when I thought I finally got through to him, the moment he looked me in the eyes right before we had sex.

The brown irises of his eyes were swimming with emotion. Emotion that I could have sworn had at least a little something to do with me. Sure, I saw the fear and uncertainty. The worry in them that he was no better than his father. It's a fear we all harbor, all three of us – Mason, Quinn, and me. But Mason, he convinced us that our lives don't have to be that way. That we hold our destiny in our own hands and can do whatever we want. Be whomever we want. We didn't have to be them. Or anything like them, for that matter.

In that moment, I thought that maybe I had done the same for him.

Maybe he had finally realized that he deserved to love and be loved.

Looking at him now, all the emotions I had tucked away for the past month rise up in me. I simultaneously want to scream at him and wrap my arms around him. Regardless of the pain I feel, seeing him again soothes something in me. There is such a familiarity, a comfort just being in the same room as him.

As much as I have missed him, I have also been dreading a moment where I would have to face him again. Like now. No matter how angry I am, no matter how hurt, I feel he just… consumes me. He tears me down and builds me up and then steals away my breath with nothing more than a look.

"Ms. McCoy, thank you so much for joining us," Lou, his agent, says to me.

Lou's a decent enough guy. Personally, I'm not a huge fan, but he's done a lot for Mason in the PR department. I just don't find him to be invested in his clients. Not the way I think he should be. The way that Coach Reed is invested in his players.

Based on the look on Lou's face, this is nothing more than him hashing out a business deal. However, when I look at Coach Reed, his face is filled with concern. He's worried about Mason. And to see him so worried, it makes me worry even more than I already am.

Coach Reed pulls me in for a hug, his arms embracing me as he greets me with a "long time, no see."

"Feels like ages," I reply with a smile on my face. "I hate to seem rude, but would someone mind telling me what I'm doing here? The suspense is killing me."

As I stand in the room, just a few feet from where Mason is seated, I can feel the weight of his stare on me. It's heavy, dark, and it has me cemented to the spot I stand in. There is no way he's sitting there silently of his own volition. Not after the numerous attempts he's made to speak to me.

"Have a seat, Avery," Coach says as he pulls out a chair for me. One that just so happens to be directly across from Mason. Great.

I take a seat but refuse to look at Mason, instead focusing my attention on Coach Reed. "So, what is it that I can do for you?"

"As I'm sure you've heard, Mason has gotten himself into a bit of trouble," his coach tells me. "We could really use your help to get him out."

I had suspected as much. Still, I'm unclear as to how or why they think I'm the solution to their Mason problem.

Coach may have phrased the sentiment as a statement; it was most definitely his way of asking if I was willing to help. It's a good question. One that I have been asking myself since Coach called. On one hand, I don't know that my heart can handle it. Yet, I can't just walk away from him when he's in trouble. He would never do that to me. So, while I feel like I'm struggling with what to do and how to respond, in my heart of hearts, I already know the answer.

No matter how angry I am. No matter how much he hurt me. I will stand by him. I will help him. Because being angry and hurt doesn't stop the fact that I love him. That I always will.

"What do you need me to do?" I ask.

"Are you fucking kidding me?" Mason shouts as he pushes away from the table. "I have tried to reach out to you for over a month. I have been fucking begging for you to listen to me for five minutes, and you wouldn't give me the time of day. Now, what, you want to step in and save me?"

"I didn't ask to come here," I say, following suit and shoving out of my chair.

He makes his way around the table and stands before me. His six-foot-four frame towers over me. Neither his height nor the angry look on his face intimidates me, though. With my hands on my hips, I stare right back at him.

"Yeah, but you sure as fuck showed up."

"To help you," I argue.

"I don't need your help."

"Are you sure about that? Because you sure as hell seem to have made a mess of everything."

Mason clenches his fists at his sides, our voices continuing to raise as we speak. Coach attempts to step between us, but Mason pushes him out of the way.

I hold up my hand, letting Coach know that I'm okay, he doesn't need to interfere. Mason would never hurt me. Not physically, at least.

"Maybe I wouldn't have if you would have just picked up your damn phone."

"You're going to blame me for the mess you created? I didn't tell you to drink and drive or fuck every woman you see."

"I haven't fucked anyone since you," he shouts.

The room goes silent. My cheeks flush, his admission in front of Lou and Coach Reed embarrassing the hell out of me and angering me at the same time.

"I'm out of here." I turn toward the door to walk away once and for all.

Mason's hand is on my arm. When I look back at him, his face is soft, his eyes welling with tears. "I'm sorry, Avery. I'm so fucking sorry."

For him to do this, to show any type of emotion in front of people, is completely out of character. The desperation he must feel for him to do it tells me just how badly he needs whatever it is they want me to do.

"What do you need me to do?" I ask.

"Just be you," Lou says.

"They want you to pretend to be my girlfriend," Mason says as he lets go of my arm. "They think having you around, people will think I'm cleaning up my act. That you make me a good guy."

The way he says it breaks my heart. "You are a good guy."

"I told them it was a stupid idea. I told them you wouldn't agree to it, but I wanted to see you, so I let them set up the meeting. I don't want you to help. I don't deserve it. I just wanted the chance to apologize face to face."

"I'll do it."

"You don't have to."

"I know."

I also know that I will never let him destroy his life, not because of his parents and not because of me.

Lou claps his hands together, clearly pleased with the success of his little plan. "We'll start moving you in today."

"Moving in?" Mason and I ask in unison.

Pretending to be Mason's girlfriend is one thing. Living with him? That is not something I am prepared nor willing to do.

"No way. No one would believe…"

"You've been friends for years. You helped him through this rough patch, saw him to the other side, and…"

"And this all just, what? Miraculously happened overnight?" I laugh at the absurdity of it. The fact that two obviously clueless men planned a romance is beyond comical. "Why don't we take it slow? A few dates, some events, then we can talk about moving in. Maybe by then, this whole thing will be cleared up and...."

"A year," Coach chimes in. "We need you to agree to this for a year."

"It's okay, Avery. Just say...." Mason speaks, but his eyes are looking at the floor.

"Three months. We don't move in together for three months. If you want people to think he's serious about this, you have to give it time. Show that it's real. Then... then I'll move in for the last nine months."

Lou and Coach Red glance between each other. "You've got a deal."

"Now, in regard to your pay..." Lou continues.

"My pay?" I say.

"Yes. Mason has agreed to cover all your tuition and expenses as well as..."

"Like hell, he will," I remark as I turn to face Mason. "I'm not doing this for money. Jesus, do you really think that little of me? I'm doing this because you're my friend, or at least you used to be."

"Avery, please. I just wanted... Fuck. I fucked everything up. I know that. But I always had every intention of taking care of you. At least... if you do this, I can still do that."

I turn to face him. "I don't need you to take care of me. I don't need you to save me. I just needed you to care about me. To be my friend."

"I do. I am. I'm trying to make this right. Trying to fix this."

"Yeah, well, you suck at it," I tell him.

His eyes lighten as I smile. "I do. But I'm trying. That has to count for something, right?"

It counts for everything.

"I have to go. I'm late for class. Just… email me the details."

Heading to the elevator, I can sense Mason behind me even before he says my name.

I don't turn. I stare at the elevator doors, my finger jabbing the button repeatedly as if it will make it come sooner.

"I know I made a mess of things. You have to know how much I care about you, though."

"Please, stop."

His body presses against my back. His lips near my ear. "I can't, Avery. I'm sorry, but I'm not giving up. I can't lose you."

The elevator doors slide open, and I hurry inside. I turn to face him, more to make sure that he isn't trying to follow me than anything.

As I stand there, my eyes meet his. I hate the emotions that looking into them stir inside me. I hate that, in this moment, I want to step into his arms and hug him, forgetting everything that happened a couple months ago.

For as much as I want that, I know I can't. I know the effect that night had on me. Then subsequently how his words tore me apart. If nothing else, being near him is just too painful.

So, then, why did I agree to this absurd plan?

Our eyes remain on each other until the doors shut.

The moment they do, my body sags against the wall.

What have I gotten myself into?

Chapter 14

Avery

"You agreed to what?" Claire exclaims.

Her astonishment is nothing compared to the humor that Quinn finds in the situation. She's seated at the table next to me, laughing hysterically.

"I agreed to pretend to be Mason's girlfriend... for a year," I reply.

Hearing me repeat the words causes Quinn to double over in laughter.

"Screw you both," I say, frustrated with the whole situation. "What was I supposed to do? Let him continue to spiral out of control?"

Both of them nod their heads.

"I love my brother, Avery, but let's face it, he can be a real ass. And you can't keep putting yourself on the line for him," Quinn tells me.

But I can. And I want to. Hell, even a part of me feels like I need to. Call it co-dependency; call it whatever you want. At the end of the day, it's just how Mason and I are.

"What exactly is this whole charade going to consist of?" Claire inquires.

"It starts with the two of you being able to keep your stupid mouths shut. Then..." I recall the message I sent Mason after the meeting.

Me: I will do this for you. But we have to do things my way.

Mason: Of course. But you don't have to do this.

Me: We need to go on a date. A nice, simple date. Dinner. Then next week – we'll do something else.

Mason: Dinner. Got it. Friday?

Me: 7

Mason: I'll pick you up.

Quinn squeals. "You two are finally going on a date."

"A pretend date," I correct her.

"You do realize who you're talking to, right?" Quinn says with a smile. Her relationship with Hunter may have started out as a charade but quickly turned into the real deal.

"That's not going to happen with us," I say.

"Stranger things have happened," Claire chimes in.

Yep, like Mason and I sleeping together. Or, like us not speaking for a month.

What a mess.

"This calls for a celebration," Quinn says as she hops up and heads to the bar.

She returns with a tray filled with shots.

I take a glass from the tray and throw it back. The more I think about my impending fake relationship, the time and energy it's going to take, the more I feel like I need a drink. And another.

"Easy girl," Claire says even though she clinks her glass with mine before doing the shot with me.

It doesn't take long before I am flying past tipsy and well on my way to full-blown drunk.

"Well, hello, ladies," a familiar voice says.

When I turn and see that it's none other than Trent standing there, I groan. "What are you doing here?"

It's a small bar near campus, usually only frequented by students. A professional athlete walking in the door isn't an everyday occurrence, and all the patrons take notice. All eyes are on us. Even in my drunken state, I'm aware enough of my surroundings to know that I need to step back put some distance between us.

"I overheard Quinn tell Hunter you guys would be coming here tonight." A cocky grin is plastered on his face. "You haven't returned any of my calls."

"I've been busy. Really busy." It's a lie, but I don't feel like getting into anything further with him right now.

His hand moves toward me, tucking a strand of hair behind my ear. "I've missed seeing you around the stadium."

"Hands off, asshole," Mason's voice booms through the bar.

Shit, shit, shit.

If people weren't looking before, they sure as hell are now. Three hulking football players are headed in our direction, and each of them looks pissed. Mason's in the lead, followed by Hunter and Ashton.

When Trent turns to face Mason, there is a smug look on his face. That's when I realize that he's here on purpose. He didn't come to see me; he came to get under Mason's skin. The pissing match, it's not one-sided. Mason's right; Trent is gunning for him. But why?

"Is there a problem?" Trent asks innocently.

Mason doesn't speak, only begins to move toward Trent with his hands clenched at his sides. I cut him off, stepping, or rather, stumbling, between the two of them.

"Don't do this. Don't act like this," I say, my eyes pleading with Mason. This is the exact kind of behavior being with me is supposed make him refrain from.

Mason looks at Trent, then back down at me. There's something in his eyes, something that I can't quite read.

Fully ready to put him in his place, his hand touches my cheek before I can speak, silencing me. His tongue darts out to wet his lips, and a second later, they cover mine. Even though I should fight it, I can't. Instinctively, my hands reach for his waist as I let him kiss the breath out of me. It's soft, gentle, nothing more than our lips pressing together, yet it still sets every piece of me on fire. When the kiss ends, he brushes his nose against mine before taking a step back.

"My problem is that you had your hands on my girl, and I am not into sharing," Mason says, a cocky smirk gracing those lips that just branded mine.

I can't even argue his words. I am his girl. Whether or not that makes me an idiot is debatable, but it's what I am. I am his, even if he isn't mine.

Trent begins to laugh. "You may have won this round, Ford. But this isn't over."

As I watch Trent walk away, looking smug as ever, I realize that Mason was right. Trent really does have it out for him. And he was using me to get to do it.

"Well, that was awkward," Quinn says, breaking the connection that Mason and I are sharing. "But, looks like the lovebirds are official."

I'm about to ask what she means until I see the group of people staring at us. The phones in their hands a clear indication that they had been snapping photos.

Mason had always managed to keep me out of the press. Even when we went out together. Now, it seems like I have no other choice to be thrust right smack dab in the middle of it. After all, that's what we're doing, isn't it? Putting on a show for the world to see? A show to prove he isn't as bad as everyone thinks he is?

Mason curses under his breath. "I'll take care of it."

"No, it's fine. I'm going to have to get used to it."

Is that even possible? I've often wondered how he did it, dealt with the limelight and the cameras. I guess I'll be finding out.

"Are you sure?" he asks. "I don't care about…"

"I know. And, yes, I'm sure."

His arm moves from me to reach for one of the shot glasses. He throws back the drink, bids us a goodnight, and heads for the door.

"Mason, wait," I call after him.

He stops before reaching the door and turns to me.

"I'm so sorry about that. Whatever it looked like, I assure you, it wasn't anything. There's nothing going on between Trent and me," I say, feeling like I need to make sure he knows that.

"You don't owe me an explanation," he tells me. While that may be true, I still find myself needing to explain.

"I won't do anything to ruin this for you," I assure him.

"You didn't do anything wrong. I'm the one that keeps fucking up."

"Like by kissing me."

Another small chuckle. "Kissing you is a lot of things, Avery. A mistake is not one of them."

"Oh," I say softly as I watch him walk out the door.

Whether it was for effect or not doesn't even matter. The moment, the kiss, it all felt real. So real that I'm fairly certain my heart is going to shatter to pieces when this all comes to an inevitable end.

Chapter 15

Mason

"Any more jealous tirades?" Hunter asks as he takes an unwelcomed seat on my couch.

The fucker has been giving me shit nonstop since the other night at the bar.

He had been the one that wanted to go there, to see Quinn. I followed because I don't have much choice. I'm trying to clean up my act, and sticking by Mr. Wonderful over here is definitely one way of doing that.

Okay, that's not completely true. I knew Avery was going to be there. And maybe she's part of the reason that I tagged along. Seeing her earlier in the day at the stadium only made me miss her that much more. What better excuse to spend some time with her than to tag along with Hunter and Ashton?

"I wasn't jealous," I argue.

"Sure, you weren't," he says with a roll of his eyes. "Just like your jealousy isn't why you keep hammering him on the field. Or why you slept with Avery in the first place."

"Fuck off," I tell him. The more I deny it, the more he's going to push. And frankly, he's not wrong. Not that I'm ready to admit that to him yet. Or anyone else, for that matter.

It's true, though; jealousy is exactly what started this. Having to see Avery with someone else made something come over me. I saw her in a new light, as something more than just my friend. Being me, I tried to dispel it, but it didn't work. It only became more and more obvious as time has gone on.

In fact, I'm fairly certain those feelings were always there. I had just always managed to restrain myself. Until that night.

"Are you sure about this?" Hunter asks. He's now leaning against the wall, his arms crossed as he gives me a look. One that speaks volumes, but I don't want to listen to.

I'm still in shock that she agreed to help. I was certain that she wouldn't. And who would have blamed her? As I stand here looking in the mirror, adjusting my hair, I try to wrap my head around the fact that it's so I can take her on a date. A fake date, but a date, nonetheless. What is even more unbelievable is the fact that I like the idea of it. Me and Avery, on a date. Something that once felt so absurd actually feels kind of right.

"Am I sure about doing what Coach and Lou want so I don't completely destroy everything I worked for? Yes. Am I sure about using Avery to do it? No." In fact, as excited as I am to spend time with her tonight, I hate that I'm essentially using her again. It's what got her into this mess in the first place. Me using her, taking advantage of her friendship and her kind heart to satisfy my own needs.

"What about..." his voice trails off, the question he's asking implied.

"I already apologized. I don't know what else to do."

"There are a million things you can do."

I turn abruptly to face him. "And I've done them. Believe me, I've fucking done them. If you have some miracle trick up your sleeve, please, let me know.

He ignores my outburst, his advice following despite knowing I don't want to hear it. "You could tell her how you feel about her."

There's an implication in his voice telling of what it is he thinks those feelings entail. And while I'm fairly certain that I know what it is, I ask anyway. "And how exactly do I feel about her, Hunt?"

"You love her. But you don't want to because you're scared. Or you don't think you deserve it." He shrugs his shoulders. "Maybe both. But I know you love her. If you didn't... losing her, wouldn't be tearing you apart the way it is."

"What's tearing me apart is the fact that I hurt her. Just like it would if I did something to hurt you," I say, trying to deflect.

"So, what you're saying is that if you hurt me, you wouldn't be able to have sex with anyone else? Weird flex, man."

"Screw you," I say, partly pissed and partly laughing. "You know what I mean."

"What I know is that since that night, you haven't been yourself. A piece of you is missing, Mase, and that piece is Avery." His hand rests on my shoulder as he looks me in the eye. "I'm grateful to be your best friend, but Avery? She owns you in a way that I never could. One that I don't want to."

"Even if..." I shake my head. Accepting my feelings for Avery and acting on them are two different things. Yes, I accept that there is more to Avery and me. No way in hell do I intend to do anything about it. Why? "She deserves better. She deserves a guy who isn't fucked up."

"You're not as fucked up as you think, man. Besides, you forget one really important detail."

I raise an eyebrow, "What's that?"

"She knows how fucked up you are, and she still likes you."

God only knows why. She's the only one in my life who has ever fully known the demons I carry with me. The fears, the nightmares. She's also the only one who knows how to ease them.

"I have to go. Don't want to be late for our first date," I say as I grab my keys and the over-the-top bouquet of flowers that I picked out for her. Purple, pink, and blue flowers with white baby's breath sprinkled throughout. Just like the corsage I bought her for our senior prom. We spent it sitting in a park on a bench, eating McDonalds, and laughing our asses off because we couldn't afford to go to the actual dance. Even without a prom dress on, she still looked gorgeous. And the smile that lit up her face when I handed her the corsage is still ingrained in my mind. As is the way she felt in my arms when she threw hers around me and hugged me to thank me for it.

I knock on the door to her apartment and groan when Quinn answers. She stands there, smiling at me.

"Don't start," I warn her.

She rolls her eyes at my warning. Despite giving it to her, I know that she's not going to heed it. Instead, I stand here, waiting for whatever it is she's about to dish out.

"You better not fuck this up. You better find a way to make her forgive you, and when she does…" I wait for her to continue because I know she isn't done with me yet. "You better hold onto her and never let her go." She presses a finger into my chest. "The two of you belong together. I know you don't see it, and I know she denies it, but it's true. Quit trying to force yourself into the friend zone when we both know that you want more."

"I…"

"Don't deserve it?" she asks, quirking an eyebrow at me. "That's garbage, and you know it. You have done nothing but sacrifice for me – and for her. You are a good guy Mason Ford if you would just get your head out of your ass and realize it."

"I was going to say that I don't remember being this harsh with you when you fucked up."

"Yeah, well, you didn't have the balls to do it. I do."

"Explains a lot about you and Hunter," I tease.

"Joke all you want, but the fact is, you know I am right."

She opens the door allowing me to step inside now that she's said her peace. As I step over the threshold, she slaps my ass. I turn to her, a very confused look on my face. "Go get your girl."

"Way too much time with Hunter," I chuckle.

The amusement subsides the minute Avery steps into focus. The sleek dress, her dark hair in loose curls falling around her shoulders. The literal girl next door turned complete sex goddess. How did I miss this before?

Or, maybe, it's just more noticeable now because I know. I have a vivid memory of exactly what is underneath that dress and how damn good it feels.

As I stare at her, words escaping me, Quinn elbows me. I need to say something before I go and fuck this up too.

"You look amazing," I tell her.

"I should; you spent a fortune on this dress. I told you this wasn't necessary," she says. "I'm perfectly capable of buying my own clothes."

"I didn't. Lou, he must have… I'm sorry," I tell her. All the while, I'm cursing Lou and whatever it is that he thinks he knows about women. Maybe it applies to other women, but not to Avery.

I've tried every way I can think of to help her, ease any financial burden, but she refuses. She works. She goes to school. She is dead set on doing this and doing it on her own even though I can make every worry disappear.

"It's fine. Do I look acceptable?" she asks.

My shoulders slump, my head lowering, a subtle shake of disbelief. "No." With my head still down, my eyes lift to meet hers. "What you look is beautiful."

"As long as you're happy," she tells me as she walks right past me.

Quinn gives my arm a soft squeeze in encouragement before she exits the room leaving Avery and me alone. As grateful as I am for her support, it's not encouragement I need. No, I need a fucking miracle.

I move closer to where Avery stands, fiddling with her purse. "I brought you these," I tell her as I extend the bouquet to her.

She scowls at the flowers, the arrangement I had hoped would bring a smile to her face. A memory from a happier time when she didn't hate me.

She sets them down and heads out the door. I follow her out of the apartment and down the hallway, where she's already waiting for the elevator.

"I brought the flowers for you, not because of some act," I say, trying to convince her that this is real. Maybe it's not a real date, but it's really me, her friend, trying to win her over because I miss the hell out of her. "And, me saying you look beautiful, it isn't a line. I mean it. You look beautiful, Avery."

She remains standing there, facing the elevator doors, willing them to open so we can step inside and get this show over with. I'm standing next to her, watching her, just grateful that she's near me again. Speaking to me. Even if she doesn't really want to be.

"Thank you."

Chapter 16

Avery

My actions back in the apartment were unnecessary. I regretted them almost immediately. It's that very behavior that's going to protect me and keep my heart safe. It's how I have to be if I have any hope of surviving this. Mason is nothing if not charming. And the sweeter he is, the harder it's going to be for me to stay mad at him.

Walls up. I constructed them to keep him out. I'm being a bitch to make sure that he doesn't knock them down.

Like with the flowers. Not only did him bringing me flowers take me by surprise, he didn't bring me just any flowers. No, he brought the exact flowers he gave me for our senior prom. The amount of restraint it took to not smile or hug him was unquantifiable. One look at those flowers today, and I could feel my resolve begin to crumble. Rather than letting him see that, I forced down the emotions and kept on walking, pretending they didn't affect me when in actuality, they shook me straight to my core.

Memories flooded me, good memories of our senior prom. A prom that neither of us attended because we couldn't afford it. Even with our lack of funds, Mason somehow managed to buy me that corsage. And a bottle of tequila. Sitting there on that park bench with him laughing and drinking… it was better than any prom experience I could have had. In fact, it is the best night I've ever had. It was perfect. I honestly don't think Mason ever fully understood how much that night meant to me or how much he means to me. Not then, and not now.

We ride to the restaurant in silence, with me staring out the window, trying to remind myself why I'm angry with him. What would normally have been a comfortable silence felt uncomfortable and awkward. I've never felt that way around Mason before. Even the first night we met, there was just this automatic level of ease. We could talk for hours, sit in silence; it didn't matter. We just enjoyed being together. And we always knew what the other needed, what they were thinking.

Now, I feel so disconnected from him. I can't read him or understand what in the hell would have possessed him to use me like that. It feels like we fell so far that even if I could forgive him, I don't know if we could ever actually be us again.

The moment the car comes to a stop, I reach for the door handle. He sets his hand on my arm. "Please, Avery. Let me?"

I retract my hand and set it in my lap as I wait for him to make his way around to my side of the car. He's going to take my hand; he's going to touch me. I know him. I know every damn move he makes. As I wait, I do my best to prepare myself for the emotions that touch is going to stir, for the hidden desire that's going to surface. When I set my hand in his, it's so much more than even that. His touch is everything. Every need, every desire, every single shred of happiness.

With my hand in his, I step from the vehicle. He pulls me against him. His smile is instantaneous and genuine where I expect it to be forced. Most people wouldn't know the difference, but I do. I want to speak, to say something, but I can't. I'm at a complete loss.

"Have you always looked like this?" The fingers that aren't intertwined with mine brush against my cheek.

"I guess I was just never worth looking at before," I say.

"That's not true. I was just too afraid to look."

I'm not sure whose benefit we're having this conversation for. The onlookers? Him? Me? Whoever it is, doesn't really matter. What matters is that we don't need to be having it because it's putting thoughts into my head that don't need to be there. Thoughts that put us in this position in the first place.

For the first time, I glance at the restaurant. Francesca's. It's a five-star Italian eatery that you can only get into if you're someone. While I am not, Mason sure as hell is. He must really be sorry because he is pulling out all the stops. I've been dying to come here, but even before we were on bad terms, he never brought me. I had assumed he hadn't been paying attention. But it looks like I was wrong. He had been. Maybe he saw more than I thought.

"You're really pulling out all the stops for this charade," I say softly.

"I'm pulling out all the stops for you, Ave."

He opens the door to the restaurant, and the moment that we step inside, the whole restaurant takes notice of the hulking football player. If Lou wanted us to be seen, he sure as hell got his wish. Everyone is looking, watching, whispering. Even more so, I'm sure, thanks to the spectacle at the bar the other night.

"I'm sorry, I know how uncomfortable this must be," he whispers in my ear.

I plaster on a huge smile and lean into him, my fingers brushing against his jaw. "This isn't my first rodeo with your stardom," I remind him.

Ever since he entered the NFL, Mason has been in the spotlight. At first, it was due to his amazing athleticism. Then his prowess with women. And now, the shit storm he's made out of his life – professionally and personally.

He wraps his arm around my waist, his hand pressing to the small of my back. "True. But before I could shelter you from it, at least a little. Now...." He glances around the room, eyes prying, pictures snapping. "Now, I'm basically feeding you to the wolves."

"I don't know about all that."

"I do. This isn't fair to you. I created this mess. I'll figure my own way out."

"No, you won't. Besides, I already signed the contract, so there's no backing out. Just... play nice," I say.

The corner of his mouth quirks up into a smile. "You don't always like it when I'm nice."

His words, the memory it stokes the flame of all things you would think he would rather forget, considering he is the one that deemed it a mistake. Yet here he is, smiling, reminiscing, hardening. Holy shit.

"Yeah, well, I sure as hell don't like being used either," I say, my fake smile still plastered on as the one on Mason's falls.

Just as he opens his mouth to speak, to refute the fact that he used me, I'm sure, the hostess arrives to escort us to our table.

She maneuvers us through the restaurant to a table in a remotely secluded section where no one will be the wiser that we aren't sitting here having an amazing time and head over heels in love with each other.

"Will this work?" she asks.

"It's perfect, thanks," Mason replies. He steps behind the chair and pulls it out for me.

I smile sweetly as I take the seat he's offering. Setting my napkin in my lap, I immediately reach for the menu and begin to study it. By study it, I mean stare at the words without actually reading them because I'm afraid to look at Mason.

"What looks good?" he asks. His voice sounds completely normal as if it's just another day in paradise. Meanwhile, here I sit with my stomach in knots, unable to speak.

Mason rests his elbows on the table and leans forward, his fingers pressing the menu down. "Will you at least look at me, please?"

My eyes flash up and glance at him before returning to the menu that he is now holding prisoner on the table. "Happy?"

He sits back in the chair and folds his arms across his chest. "In case you haven't noticed, I haven't been happy for quite some time."

"And that's my fault?" I ask, my eyes finally meeting his.

"No, it's mine. But you won't... What do I have to do, Avery? What will make this better?" He runs a hand through his meticulously, disheveled head. "You know how I feel about you. You know what you mean to me.

And yes, I made a mistake. I just need you to tell me how to fix it."

Hearing him call our night together a mistake only solidifies how I already feel. If only I hadn't agreed to this stupid charade, I would be able to keep my distance. I wouldn't be risking my heart – again.

"Like you said, it was a mistake. We already made it. There's no fixing it," I tell him.

"Like hell there isn't," he says, his hand slamming down onto the table.

The sound startles me, causing my body to nearly jump out of my seat. My eyes dart around the room, trying to determine if anyone saw anything. The last thing we need is to draw negative attention to us. How are we going to portray the perfect couple when we can't even look at each other?

"I refuse to believe that this is it, that this is as good as it gets," he says.

"It's all I can give you."

"Then we're done here," he tells me.

"Excuse me?"

"I said, we're done here. We're leaving. I'm not doing this."

"You don't have a choice."

"Like hell I don't. I am not going to spend the next year sitting next to you and not speaking to each other. It's fucking ridiculous."

"Fine. I'm sorry. We'll talk, okay?"

He shoves away from the table and stands. "No. It's not good enough."

"Sit down," I order him.

He presses his hands onto the table. "I am not going to put you through this. You hate me so much that you haven't even been able to look at me all night. It's not worth it."

"I'll do better," I tell him.

He shakes his head. "I don't want you to do better. I want things to actually *be* better. But that's not going to happen. Is it?"

Every part of me wants to scream yes and tell him that we'll be okay. I can't though. I can't let him back in. I can't put myself through the inevitable heartache that will bring me. "No."

"Then we're done here. Let's go."

Before he can move, I set my hand on his. "Wait."

My touch seems to calm the frustration and anger raging inside him. "Things will never be like they were, but... maybe.... I'll try, Mason. I'll really try."

It's a ploy. Nothing more than a way to get him to stay. And it works.

He returns to his seat, his eyes steadfast on me and his hand holding mine. "I will do whatever it takes, Avery. I just don't want to lose you."

"Then let's have dinner," I say. I make sure not to make any promises, not to agree to let him not lose me. Because as soon as this year is up, we're done.

The letter Quinn handed me the other day sealing that fate.

One year and then I can leave Remington and Mason behind.

Chapter 17

Avery

"You haven't said one word about your date the other night," Quinn badgers me.

She's been asking nonstop and apparently isn't grasping what my silence on the matter means.

"Oh, come on. This isn't fair," she pouts. "Please, Avery?"

I stop in the middle of the walkway, the spot where we take separate paths every Tuesday as we head to different parts of campus.

I'm not sure exactly what she's looking for. Mason and I muddled our way through dinner, and he walked me back to my apartment. He stepped inside for a moment only so if anyone were watching, it would appear that we wanted some privacy for a good-bye. That was it.

The conversation that we kept was minimal. It barely scratched the surface of anything outside of the weather.

"What do you want to know, Quinn?" I ask, my voice laced with irritation.

"Did you guys make up?" Her voice is soft as she asks the question, almost childlike.

For as messed up as we are, Mason and I essentially took over the role of parents to Quinn. None of us had parents that were worth a damn, and Quinn, well, she had no concept of what one even was. He was angry and hurt, but Mason said that changed when I started to come around. Hearing her sound like this, the sadness in her voice, it breaks my heart.

"No," I reply. "I told him I would try, though."

Here I am lying to Quinn now, too. Because while I am going to try to help Mason repair his reputation, that's as far as it's going to go. Last night only proved to me how much being around him affects me. How much my heart would break if I returned to the way things were. At the end of the day, it's not just Mason that I'm angry with. It's myself. I let this happen. I consented to everything. And the fact that my heart is broken, well, that's not his fault. It's mine.

Mason and me, we're friends. Nothing more. I have known my entire life exactly where I stood with him. And yet, somehow, I let my feelings for him escalate. All the way, to the point that I fell in love with him like a damn idiot. An idiot who knew better.

It wasn't exactly something I could control. Hell, I did my best to fight it for as long as I could. While I was perfectly capable of pushing those feelings to the side and ignoring them as his friend, us having sex opened a world that I wasn't ready for. It gave me insight into a place I never imagined being a part of. It gave me hope.

Only to have it torn away by his words.

"I know this is more than him just being a jerk. I know why what he said upset you so much. I also know that him going to you, what happened between you, it is more to him than you know. Just... be patient. Take this time to show him exactly what it could be like if you two were together."

"I appreciate the sentiment."

"It's more than that, Ave. It's me knowing both of you. It's me being in the middle, hearing both sides of every detail of your friendship. You are everything to Mason. I just don't think that he quite understands what that means. Show him."

"I'll think about it."

"That's all I ask," she says with a smile that tells me she thinks she's won. "Besides, how great would it be if you two did end up together and we became real sisters?"

I pull her in for a hug. "We are real sisters. You and Mason are the only family I want."

Her head tilts to the side, her eyes imploring me to hear the words I just said.

"I hate you," I say without conviction.

"Love you too… sis." She gives me one last squeeze before heading off in the direction of her class.

My lecture, the one that I should be paying attention to if I have any hope of ever becoming a licensed physical therapist, does not have my attention. Quinn's words, her implication that maybe I should take this opportunity to give things with Mason a shot without him even realizing it, however, do. They're all I think about through class, through Professor Peters calling on me to answer a question that I didn't even hear.

"I'm sorry, I uh… what was the question?" I ask, hoping he doesn't call me out like I've heard him do to others.

He's a tough professor, and I've been his prize student until recently. My grades haven't slipped terribly, and while most professors wouldn't have noticed, he did.

"Are you too busy daydreaming about your date with the football player to pay attention to my lecture?" he asks.

I guess he's seen the photos that I have been ignoring. Not because the photos concern me, but because the comments linked to them do. The ones that say I'm not good enough for Mason. That I'm too fat. Not pretty enough. One look was more than enough.

"I'm sorry, what was the question?"

He glances down at his watch and then back up at me. "Lucky for you, class is over."

Embarrassed by my recent slip in his class, I gather my things in hopes of rushing out the door. No sooner is my notebook in my bag do I hear him call my name.

I blow out a breath as I make my way down the stairs to him. "Yes, sir?"

"Is everything okay, Avery?" he asks, genuine concern in his voice.

"Yes, sir. I'm sorry I was distracted in class today. I'll do better." Seems I've been promising that to a lot of people lately.

"It's not just today, Avery," he says, handing me a sheet of paper. It's my latest exam. One that I got a B on. To most, a B is great. But for me? In Professor Peter's class?

"I've had a lot going on and… I'm sorry."

"If you need to talk, I'm here. You're my best student, Avery. I don't want to see this again."

I nod. "You won't. I promise."

"Enjoy your day then. And study, will you?"

"I will. Thank you."

No sooner do I step into the sunshine; I step directly into Mason.

His presence startles me. I let out a slight scream, the impact from walking into him throwing me off balance.

"Woah, hey there," he says, his hands gripping my arms to steady me. "Everything okay?"

No, nothing has been okay for a long time now. The ramifications of all of it finally starting to take its hold on me. Especially after our dinner that night. The way he stared at me all through dinner. The things he said and did. Every bit of it a perfect date, if I hadn't been so hell bent on making sure it wasn't.

"Yeah, you just surprised me. What are you doing here?" I ask as I step out of his hold. The physical connection too much for me to bear at the moment.

"There are a few things we need to discuss. I figured working them out in person would be better than Lou sending you an email telling you what to do," he says.

"Oh, okay. What is it?"

"Can I buy you lunch?" he asks.

My instinct is to say no to try and keep our interactions to a minimum. But I remind myself that this is my duty now. I agreed to play Mason's girlfriend without taking into consideration of the damage it would do to my heart. There's a contract and everything.

"Sure," I reply, trying to hide my frustration.

His eyes widen; clearly, he's stunned by my sudden change of heart. "Yeah, great. You want to go somewhere? Or stay on campus? We can do whatever you want."

"Probably best if we stay on campus. More visibility." It's a younger crowd. A crowd that would be much more likely to snap photos and post them to Instagram or TikTok, or wherever they see fit.

"I don't care about the visibility."

"Isn't that the whole reason we're doing this?" I ask. Mason's face falls, and he looks more like a little boy whose puppy got kicked than an adult man. "We could grab something from the cafeteria and eat outside?"

"Whatever you want," he says, reaching for my hand, but I tug it away and instead hold tightly onto the strap of my bag.

"So, uh, are there a lot of events coming up?" I ask.

"A few," he replies as he shoves his hands in his pockets. "A couple charity things, a golf outing. Nothing crazy."

"No problem, that's what I'm here for," I tell him.

Just as we're about to enter the cafeteria, I misstep and fall into his arms for the second time today. His hands are gripping me a little firmer this time, my body resting flush against his.

"Easy there." There's a smile on his face. "I'm used to girls falling at my feet, but this is a bit much Ave."

For a moment, I forget. I forget why we're here, why I'm angry, and most of all, why we're so messed up. Just for that moment, I focus on Mason. My friend. My partner in crime.

As we stand there, he tucks a strand of hair behind my ear. "I've missed you, Ave."

Being here with him like this, the gentle touch, his words washing over me it does things to my heart and my body that I'm not entirely sure I can handle. Speechless, I stand there staring at him, unsure what to do or where to go from here. It's not until he snakes his hand around to the back of my neck that I realize what's happening. He's kissing me. And my walls are crumbling down.

When he breaks the kiss, he locks eyes with me, his fingers brushing over his own lips. "God, I've missed you."

I take the moment for what it is. Sex and physicality are never an issue for Mason. It's everything else that's the problem.

"We should probably grab lunch," I say as I slowly pull out of his hold. "I have another class soon."

Mason remains still for a moment, and I'm fearful he'll start an argument that would inevitably create a scene. He doesn't though. He just opens the door for me and allows me to step through.

As I do, I hear him mumble, "This isn't over."

Pretending not to hear, I continue walking, acting completely oblivious to the mixed signals he's giving me.

Chapter 18

Mason

I can't even fight it anymore.

I tried. God knows, I tried. Every time I see Avery, I just can't resist.

Keeping my feelings hidden was for her benefit. My sole purpose to protect her from what a shit show I am.

No matter how much I care about her, the fact of the matter is I don't know how to. I don't know how to be the man she deserves. Hell, I don't even know how to be a boyfriend.

Instead, I focus on repairing our friendship.

Or, at least, that's what I try to do.

Every time I'm near her, the need to touch her, to kiss her, it's undeniable. And, apparently, unstoppable. Because I lose all control. Every ounce flies out the window the minute I look at her, and all I want is more.

I don't deserve it, but fuck if I don't want it.

The question is, what do I do? Do I keep going on like I am, trying to be her friend and ignoring the feelings I have? Or do I tell her, pursue her, and risk our entire relationship on something that I may very well suck at?

"You okay?" Hunter asks when I step up to my locker.

"Nope."

"Avery?"

"Yep."

Hunter scrubs his hand over his face. "What now?"

He asks the question as if he's already resigned to the fact, I must have done something wrong. It's not a wrong assumption to make; still, it hurts.

"I don't know what to do," I say. It's not much, but it's the start of my admission.

"What you need to do is quit lying to yourself. You need to accept how you feel about Avery and do something about it before it's too late." I open my mouth to argue, but the look on his face tells me to just shut up and listen. So, I do. I owe him at least that much. "Listen, I get why you have this no attachment, no relationship rule, okay? I saw how you grew up. I know what you had to deal with. And I know why it all seems like nothing but a crock of shit to you. But… it's real. And it's amazing. And I promise you, it's exactly what you're feeling for Avery."

"I know," I admit.

His eyes get wide, and he's looking at me like I've grown another head. "You know?"

I nod my head. "It took me losing her to realize it, but yeah, I know how much Avery means to me. I know that she's it. There's no one else who will ever matter to me the way she does."

Hunter's smiling now, but I can see the confusion on his face. "Then what's the problem?"

"What isn't the problem? Let's face it, this shit is all new to me. What if I can't give her what she needs? She deserves better than what I can give her."

"Better than what? Fuck, Mase, I don't know how many times I have to say this to get it through your head – you are not him."

"How can you be so sure? Look at me, look at what I've done," I say, referring to the mess that is currently my life.

"What exactly have you done that's so terrible, Mase? Sowed your wild oats? Became a damn good football player? Or, how about the fact that you busted your ass to become something from nothing? Quit giving yourself the shit end of the stick. Quit thinking you're him. You're not. You are so much damn better, and you prove it every day by how you take care of your sister; what a great friend you are to Avery and me."

I cock my head to the side. He can't be serious? After what I did to Avery? I am far from a good friend.

"You know I'm right. Yes, you've gone about all of this in a fucked up roundabout way, but who cares. It got you to where you need to be. You know how you feel about her, and now it's time you do something about it."

"Thanks for the pep talk, but…"

"Christ, man, you need to find a way to deal with your shit because if you don't, you might throw away the one thing that makes you happy."

"It's just… even if you're right and I'm not like my father, I'm still not entirely sure that I deserve her."

How could I after everything I've done? Every woman I've scorned? How in the hell could I deserve someone as good and kind as Avery?

"You don't," Hunter deadpans.

"What the fuck?" I ask, laughter bubbling over.

His hand squeezes my shoulder. "You don't deserve her any more than I deserve Quinn, but we're lucky fuckers because they want us."

"Are you sure, man? That she wants me? Because…"

"I'm positive. And if you need someone else to corroborate that, just ask Quinn and Claire."

Maybe we are meant to be.

If I thought my mind was fucked before, it's nothing compared to what it is now after my conversation with Hunter. There's so much to consider. Even more that I need to figure out before I can even attempt to tell her anything. For the first time in what feels like forever, though, I feel like a weight has been lifted off me. While I know I still have a long way to go in figuring my shit out, I finally have a moment of clarity.

I focus on practice, the new drills Coach has us doing. And I fucking rock it. It's about damn time too.

"Now, that's what I want to see," Coach Reed says as we make our way back in the locker room.

"Thanks, Coach," I reply.

Despite my shit mood earlier, the productive practice is making me feel alive again. Trent staying out of my way today made it all that much better.

Coach pulls me to the side. "How is everything else?"

He wants to know is how things are between Avery and me. I wish I had better news for him. And for me too. "She hasn't killed me yet," I say with a shrug. "It's a start."

"That it is, kid. That it is," he says, chuckling as he walks away.

When I make it back to my place, I'm exhausted and sore. The last thing I expect is to find Avery standing at front of my door. My smile at seeing her there is automatic.

"Hey, everything okay?" I ask as I approach her.

She looks nervous standing there. Almost as if she's unsure if she's welcome or not.

"Yeah. I uh... I'm not really sure why I came here."

"Okay." I push the door open. "Well, do you want to come in and be unsure?"

She takes her lip between her teeth as she contemplates what her answer should be. I've seen her do this a million times. My reaction to it is definitely different than it used to be.

"It would probably look weird if I didn't," she says.

Personally, I don't really give a damn what it does or doesn't look like. The thing I care about is getting her to come inside and take a step in a positive direction. One that I hope is the start to us repairing our friendship.

"Probably," I agree as I hold the door open for her.

Step through Avery. Come inside. Let me fix this.

She steps inside, but her feet remain cemented to the floor near the door, her hands folded in front of her.

"You good, or did you want to come in more? I won't bite," I lean in close to her, my lips at her ear. "Unless you want me to."

"You can be a real ass sometimes, you know that?" She tries to sound angry, but I can see the smile she's trying to hide as she walks further into the house. She even manages to set her purse down on the table before crossing her arms and glaring at me.

"Pretty sure we've established that already."

"I guess I was just wondering about tomorrow. If there is anything specific I should know?"

"Nah," I say as I head toward the kitchen. It's an attempt to draw her in further. Maybe, she'll even give me that five minutes that I need to explain.

Not that I have a damn clue what I want to say to her or how to explain it. Seriously don't think "I have feelings for you, but I don't get them, and I'm not sure what to do about them" is going to make anything better. Worse, maybe. Definitely not better.

A moment later, she storms into the kitchen. "You can't just keep kissing me like that."

I'm taken off guard by her statement. Of all the things she could possibly yell at me for, I didn't think that would be it.

"Why not?"

"Because…"

I wait. "Because why?"

"Because…" I continue to wait, a smirk spreading on my lips. "Because…"

"Can't think of a reason, can you?"

"Because it's not okay."

"Funny, the way I see it, you're my girlfriend, and that makes it more than okay. In fact, I'm pretty sure it means that I should do it again."

I make my way around the island to the side where she's standing.

"No." She presses her hand to my chest as she speaks. She says the word, but there is no conviction behind it.

"Please?" I won't take what she isn't offering. Every damn piece of her is screaming that she wants more except what I actually need to move forward – her words.

"Tell me I can kiss you, Ave. Tell me you want me too."

"I don't," she says, her body trembling under my touch.

"Are you sure about that?"

"Why are you doing this?" she asks. She's backed herself up against the wall, my hands pressed against it on either side of her head.

I move in closer, my lips a whisper away from hers. "Because."

"Ugh," she groans as she tries to push me away.

"Because," I say again. "I can't stop wanting you. Or thinking about you. Christ, Ave, I don't know what the fuck I'm feeling, but it's all for you."

She shakes her head, refusing to hear me. Refusing to believe me.

"It's true." My lips brush against hers. "You taste so damn good." My hand slides down her body. "You feel so damn good."

"You're…"

"I'm what?"

My lips are so close to hers, able to feel her breaths, close enough to capture. My hand slides under the material of her shirt to her breast. She arches into me.

"You like that?"

Her only response is a sharp intake of air as my thumb flicks over her nipple.

"Tell me, Ave. Tell me what I need to hear."

"I want…" The phone in her pocket begins to ring. "I have to get that."

I back away, allowing her the space to answer her phone. Its' also just enough time and distance to end whatever we had started.

"I have to go," she tells me.

"Not even going to give me the chance to persuade you to stay?"

A small smile. A slight shake of her head.

I shrug. "Can't blame a guy for trying."

Following her to the door and into the hallway, my eyes are glued to her as she steps into the elevator. "Night, Ave."

There's that ghost of a smile again. Hopefully, another chink in the armor gone. "Goodnight, Mason."

Chapter 19

Avery

Mason offers his hand to me to help me out of the limo, but I refuse to take it. Instead, I step out on my own and clutch my purse in front of me. Before Mason arrived to pick me up for tonight's event, I made sure to re-erect the walls he had begun to tear down. After the events of the past couple of weeks, my head is all over the place. Things Mason has been saying, the kisses for no one's benefit but our own. It's making my head jump to conclusions that I know aren't real. I reminded myself how badly this would all end and how much my heart would break.

In order to do that, I needed to keep my distance. Not an easy feat considering we are supposed to be dating and in love.

Mason's hand skims across the skin on my bare back. The touch sends a shiver up my spine. I knew this dress was a bad idea. Too much exposed skin for him to touch. To sear. To weaken me and cause me to crumble.

I can't let him touch me. I can't let my resolve deteriorate any more than it already has. Hell, a huge piece of it did when I not only ended up on his doorstep but almost let him kiss me. No, I need to keep my distance in order to keep my emotions in check.

Allowing my feet to move faster, I quicken my pace as I enter the building before him. My getaway doesn't go unnoticed, and Mason is clearly not pleased with it. His large, strong hand grabs my arm and pulls me into an empty hallway.

His eyes pierce me, hold me there against my will with just a look. What comes next is the last thing I expect. "Are you sure you want to do this?"

"Of course, I do. I agreed to it, didn't I?"

He scrubs his hand over his face. "I know what you agreed to. What I'm asking is if you want to?"

"Same thing," I argue.

"Not even close. Seriously, Ave, if you don't want to go through with this, you don't have to."

"Where is this coming from? What did I do wrong?"

Mason steps closer, invading my space, chipping away another piece of that wall around my heart. The one I constructed because of him. "You haven't done anything wrong. That's not what I'm saying."

"Then what are you saying?"

Confusion has been a constant lately. Every touch, every look, another signal for me to misconstrue. Just like I did that night. The look in his eyes that I swore was love. The emotion that I swore was directed at me. It wasn't real. None of it was real.

It was all fake. Just like this relationship we're in.

"I'm saying you don't have to do it at all. Any of it. You can walk right out that door, and I will have my driver take you home."

Thinking I want to distance myself from him, knowing it's what's best is completely different than actually doing it. Now that he's put it out there, I realize that walking away isn't what I want either.

Hell, I don't know what I want. Or what I should do. So, I do the only thing I can think of. I loop my arm through his and say, "I want to be here."

I want to be with him.

I can keep denying it all I want, but it's the truth. Regardless of how much distance I put between us or how many times I try to push him away, there is one thing that never changes. I want Mason Ford.

I have a year. A year to take this sham of a relationship and enjoy it for what it's worth. Enjoy him.

And, when it's all over, I'll be gone. I'll move on. I won't have any other choice.

"You mean it?" His voice is filled with hope. Hope that I've forgiven him. Hope that things are back to the way they used to be.

"I do," I say. The most honest words I've spoken in a long time.

There is no place I would rather be than on Mason Ford's arm.

If only it was real.

As we step into the ballroom, all eyes fall on us. I hold onto him a little tighter, squeezing the bicep that my arm is looped through. "Showtime."

"This isn't a show, Ave." His voice is smooth and calm. His eyes filled with lust and emotion again. So much that my head starts to spin.

I suppose I need to get used to it. If I'm going to play the game, I need to put my game face on.

That's exactly what I do. I smile. I hold tightly against him. I gush to anyone who asks about how amazing he is.

Countless people approach us. Some to chat up Mason and thank him for his huge donation. Others simply because they're trying to get a closer look at the new couple. Either way, the fake pleasantries and continuous smiling begins to wear on me pretty early on. Mason, on the other hand, is killing it. It's like some innate natural ability he has. And he looks damn good doing it too.

Women stare at us. The daggers they're shooting my way are fierce and unrelenting. The more people stare, the more uncomfortable I get. The more uncomfortable I am, the more I fidget.

The upside to all of it? Mason knows it. He knows I'm struggling, and he quickly ends his conversation.

"I'm thirsty. You thirsty?" Mason asks.

I nod my head in response to his question and smile when he laces his fingers with mine as we make our way to the bar.

Mason signals the bartender and orders us each a glass of champagne.

"A toast," Mason says as he holds up his glass.

"What are we toasting?"

"New beginnings." His eyes are dark and intense as he clinks his glass to mine.

"What kind of new beginnings?"

His eyes remain locked on me as he finishes his champagne. "Let's dance."

Mason hates dancing. The fact that he would even suggest it takes me by surprise. "You want to dance?"

"You sound surprised." With my hand still in his, he twirls me around before pulling me to him, his hands coming to rest on my hips. "Do I really look like a guy who could resist having a beautiful woman in his arms?"

I swallow the lump that forms in my throat at his words. His words instill emotions and hope in me, and I have to remind myself that this is just an act. It's all for show.

If that's what he wants, that's what I'm going to give him. One hell of a show.

I flash him a sexy smile as my hand reaches up to his cheek. The feeling of the scruff along his jawline sends a shudder down my spine. "You really want to dance with me?" He nods his head. "Prove it."

His fingers dig into my flesh as he stares at me with such intensity, I have to will my knees not to buckle. "Lead the way."

My body turns toward the dance floor, and I begin to walk away. His hands, however, refuse to let me get too far. They remain on me, warm and possessive.

We step onto the floor he pulls me against him. He holds me there, chest to chest, tightly pressed against each other.

"Your heart is racing," he says as we sway to the melody of the music.

Racing? It feels like it's about to burst right out of my chest. I'm nervous, and him being able to sense that only makes it worse. Rather than respond like a logical person, I giggle like a damn schoolgirl.

Mason emits a deep throaty chuckle. "You okay over there?"

"I'm fine. I just…keep dancing."

His hold on me tightens as the heat of his breath tickles my neck. "You like that?"

"Maybe," I say, teasing him.

"You ain't seen nothing yet," he proclaims. Just as I'm about to ask what exactly he wants to show me, he twirls me out then pulls me back until I'm flush against him. "Impressive, huh?"

"Very."

"You know, I think Coach was right," Mason says as he abruptly changes the subject.

"About what?"

"He said that no one would ever believe that anyone besides you would actually want to date me."

Though he's laughing, the comment makes my heart break for him. I wonder if he truly believes that. Does he think that he's unlovable for some reason?

"That, is not true."

"Women think they want me, but they don't know me. They don't know who I really am, just what they see on TV or read in the tabloids. Except you. You know every single dirty secret about me."

"And you know mine," I remind him.

"Maybe it goes both ways, then."

"What does?"

"Maybe we really are it for each other."

His words cause my feet to still, my body to freeze.

"I need some air," I tell him as I pull out of his hold. Grateful that he doesn't fight me, I head straight out the door onto the patio.

"Here," Mason's deep voice says from behind me.

When I turn to face him, he's standing there with a glass of champagne extended to me.

My hand reaches for the glass, but he pulls it back. "Under one condition."

I blow out a breath of frustration. "What?"

"You tell me why you ran."

"I'm not thirsty," I say before turning my back to him and trying to focus on the view before me.

It's an unsuccessful attempt. One that becomes even more impossible when I feel him close to me, his front touching my back. Mason picks up a piece of my hair and twirls it around his finger. "Was it because you got... overheated?"

"You want to know why? Because you just... you just keep saying things that you shouldn't. Things that make this harder than it has to be."

"I'm not sure what you're referring to."

"We're it for each other? Really Mason? We both know that even if you were interested in something – you wouldn't be interested in a woman like me."

Mason closes the gap between us, his hand moving behind my neck, his head dipping down to me, lips no more than a breath away from mine. "Is that so? If that were the case, do you think that we would have had se..."

I cover his mouth with my hand. "Shhhh." As I try to silence him, I feel his lips curve into a smile against my hand.

His grip on me tightens as he pulls me closer. There is nothing between us but my hand against his mouth, which he gently removes. His lips slide against mine, soft and tender. It's the kind of kiss that speaks of romance and promises – promises that I know he can't make. Or won't, but either way, it's more than my heart can handle.

"You need to quit doing that," I mutter.

"Why's that?"

"Because this isn't real and that kiss…"

"Felt real?" he asks.

I nod in response.

"Maybe that's because…"

"There they are," Lou's loud voice boasts, causing me to jump from Mason's hold. "The happy couple."

This time, I'm grateful for the interruption. One that pulls Mason's attention off me and onto Lou and whatever sports related thing he's babbling about. Even when they're done chatting, the heavy, sexually electrified moment that Mason and I shared is gone.

Chapter 20

Mason

A kiss.

A fucking kiss from the woman is all it takes to send me over the edge.

Not just any kiss. No. It's Avery's kiss. It's her that sends me over the edge and straight into a free-fall. I'll be damned if I would have it any other way.

The minute my lips touched hers, I was rock fucking solid. Thank God for the tux coat covering up my very untimely and unfortunate erection. I had been fighting the thing all night. The moment she stepped into the hallway, the curve hugging blue dress might not have shown much skin in the front, but in the back… Jesus. Every inch of her back was exposed. My fingers dying to touch it, to trace the lines of every bone, every muscle straight down to the swell of her ass.

When I told her she looked beautiful, her cheeks flushed, and her eyes diverted to the ground. She was downright bashful about the simplest of compliments, and fuck if that innocent look wasn't a turn on itself. I had wanted to kiss right then and there but knew I couldn't.

As much as I want her, as much as I care about her, I'm still struggling. Trying to figure out what in the hell to do about her and me and us.

Thinking about her like this is bad enough. If I act on it? Then I better fucking make sure I know what I'm doing because I can't risk losing her again.

That's what I need to do. I need to get my shit together and figure out what exactly I intend to do about them.

Can I be that man?

Can I be her man?

What I shouldn't be doing is standing here, in my shower, with my left hand pressed against the wall and my right hand jerking off my cock while I think about her. Her legs, the way she would look with her lips wrapped around my cock. Each visual, each thought making my balls tighten more.

Visions of her beneath me, her on top of me, her smiling back at me.

The memories of our night together and the intense orgasm that she pulled from me.

I move my hand over my cock faster and harder. The pressure is becoming too much to contain, the desire for her consuming me.

I need my release.

I need Avery.

The only woman I want to bury my dick in for as long as I love, I mean live. Fucking hell…

My orgasm hits me hard. Pent up desires and emotions pouring out of me.

And when I'm done. When I've released every damn ounce of cum, I slam my fist against the wall, pissed at myself. Pissed for adding her to my playbook. Pissed for turning her into spank bank material. Pissed that I may never be able to fucking have her again.

Chapter 21

Avery

Mason's fingers are laced with mine as we enter the charity golf event.

The charity gala last week was beautiful. But this is more my speed. Mason's, too. The atmosphere is much more relaxed, and a sense of ease washes over me as I see everyone milling about laughing and drinking. And it's only eight in the morning.

"Are you sure you don't want to play?" Mason asks for the millionth time.

"I suck at golf, you know that."

"I mean, yeah. But it's pretty funny to watch you play." My elbow connects with his side playfully. It's a far cry from where we were even a week ago.

Since the event, we've seen each other three times. In none of those occurrences did either of us mention our almost kiss. In fact, we didn't really mention anything about that night. Though, we did somehow still manage to find our footing a little. We're a far cry from where we were before everything went down, but it's a much more familiar territory for us.

At least we were speaking. And laughing.

Like now as he fakes pain to his side where my elbow hit him.

As we approach the registration booth, my eyes gravitate to a group of women standing off to the side. "The wives club." The women of the players, girlfriends, wives, friends with benefits, whatever they are, they always seem to stick together. They always managed to push me out.

I didn't fit the bill; I get it. I was friend zoned. With their eyes on us now, I begin to get nervous. The questions that I'm sure they're going to ask weighing on me before I even make my way over.

"I suppose I should tend to my duties," I say.

Mason notices the change in my demeanor. "There aren't any expectations, you know. They're only doing that because they don't want to play." He points out where some of the players and their significant others are already hopping onto their golf carts and heading out onto the course. "Personally? I would much prefer for you to spend the day with me."

"It would definitely give us the exposure that you need," I say.

Mason closes his eyes for a moment, and when he reopens them, they are filled with so much emotion. He steps closer to me, his fingers brushing against my cheek. "I don't give a damn about exposure or what anyone sees or thinks. I just want to be with you." He pauses before adding, "I miss you, Ave."

My shoulders sag, and my heart melts. In a moment of weakness, the admission falls so easily from my lips. "I miss you, too."

A corner of his mouth tugs up into a half-smile.

"Why are you smiling?"

"You just said you missed me. That's what I like to call progress."

"Oh really?" I ask him, laughter following suit.

He puts his arm around my shoulders as we begin to walk toward an open golf cart. "Yep. You went from hating me to missing me. Maybe, one day, you'll even forgive me."

"Don't hold your breath," I reply through my smile.

"It won't be long. I can see the chinks in the armor starting to crack."

"You must be having vision issues. All my armor is fully intact."

"Oh, is it now?"

A mischievous grin spreads across his chiseled face. I know that look. I know it means trouble.

"Mason? What are you up to?"

Before I can move, Mason grabs me, sweeping me into his arms before tossing me over his shoulder.

It all happens so quickly that I can't manage anything more than a squeal of delight.

Once I'm bent over his shoulder, I finally regain my senses. "Put me down."

"Not a chance in hell," he says as his hand connecting with my ass cheek.

"Mason." I use his name as a scolding, though I must admit I liked the feeling of his hand spanking me a little more than I ever thought I would.

"It's your fault for wearing these shorts. And having that amazing ass."

It's not until we reach the golf cart that he finally sets me down. I almost wish he would have just dropped me on my ass. Instead, he slides my body down his, slowly. With our bodies connected, we stand there next to the golf cart staring at each other. There are so many questions in his eyes, so much angst and unsureness.

"What, Mason? What is it?" I implore him because the intensity of this moment, of the look in his eyes, it's too much to not be real.

"Hey, Mason," a bubbly voice calls out.

I cringe at the familiarity of it; Crystal Mayweather, the team's head of public relations. And a former "friend" of Mason's.

My body tenses at the sight of her. Every insecurity I have ever felt on heightened awareness. Crystal is stunning. Hands down, the most beautiful woman I ever laid eyes on, and I instantly want to pull my shorts down and cover my thick thighs so no one can compare them to her long, slender ones.

Mason waves to her but immediately turns his attention back to me. He gestures his hand toward the golf cart. "Shall we?"

"Yeah, I guess," I say as I slide into the seat.

He rests his hand on the roof, his fingers touching my face, turning me, so I'm forced to look at him. "You okay?"

"Never better," I lie.

He sees right through it. I know it. He knows it. Thankfully, he doesn't push. He just nods and gets in on the other side.

We're on our third hole, and I've yet to hit the ball. I'm starting to think I would have been better with the wives' club; at least it would be less embarrassing than the way I'm playing.

"Here, let me help you," Mason says as he steps behind me.

"I'm fine," I tell him when I feel the heat of his body against mine.

"While that's true, your golf skills could use some work."

His arms wrap around me. The strong hands that months ago palmed my breasts now slide gently down my bare arms to my hands. He takes another step toward me, his body now flush against mine.

As we stand there, Mason holds me, his deep voice giving me instruction and his dick hardening and pressing against my ass. My body tenses as I gasp at the realization of what's happening.

"Sorry," he says. The apology is fake. He's not sorry.

"Crystal will do that to a guy," I say, trying to sound flippant even though the idea of him and her is currently nauseating me.

"Crystal? This isn't because of Crystal. This is all you and these damn shorts you're wearing," he tells me as he adjusts his stance, his erection harder and more firmly pressed against me.

"Oh." It's all I say because I can hear the sincerity in his voice, his hardness against my backside, and feel the way his hand in now splayed across the bare skin of my stomach beneath my shirt.

His fingers dance over my skin a moment longer before returning to the golf club.

"Ready?" He's asking if I'm ready to swing. The yes that I manage to pant out is answering a whole different question.

I can hear him emit the slightest bit of laughter.

With his hands and his body guiding mine, we swing. For the first time today, my club connects with the small ball. My body stills as I watch in shock as it glides through the air. Utterly elated, I turn and jump into Mason's arms and hug him. His arms feel like heaven wrapped around me, and as I revel in them, I realize I can't be doing this. Sure, it looks good for our little charade, but it's wreaking havoc on my heart.

Only when I try to pull away, Mason holds tighter. "I'm not ready to let go yet. I don't know if I ever will be."

I can hear the suggestion in his words, the things I begged him not to keep saying. "Yeah, well, I think we need to move onto the next hole."

Mason's eyebrows shoot up, his familiar playboy smirk on his face. "I'm game."

"Ugh," I groan as I march back to the golf cart.

Chapter 22

Mason

Today has been a perfect day. The weather is beautiful, I have Avery by my side, and Trent isn't anywhere in sight. What could be better?

There was that one moment where she let me help her with her golf swing. Our bodies pressed against each other.

No matter how much I keep telling myself that I should stay away from her, shouldn't pursue something that I don't understand, I also can't seem to resist. Everything about her draws me in. More than anything, I feel like a damn fool for not having realized it sooner.

I might be battling these feelings, trying to understand them, but there is no denying they're there. Not anymore. Not after that kiss. After how my body reacted to hers.

The idea of losing her had consumed me for so long that the possibility of us wasn't really a thought. Sure, Hunter and Quinn brought it up continuously, but aside from shooting them down, I didn't give it much more thought. After the other night, though….

I tried to not think about her. Or about us. But the more I tried to convince myself otherwise, the more I realized how impossible it was. Everything goes back to her. Every single good thing in my life begins with her.

Why shouldn't it end there too?

For reasons that I'm not sure I will ever comprehend, Avery loves me. She wants me. All of me.

And if I want to keep her in my life, I'm going to need to do something about it. Something fucking drastic.

It's high time I get off my ass, quit letting my past project onto my future. Do I believe in love and happily ever after? Not really. What I do believe in is Avery and our connection. I know with certainty that my life isn't shit without her in it.

Today, with just the two of us, things seemed to slip back into more familiar territory. There was the teasing, the smiles, and the laughter. She was playful when she desperately wanted to be standoffish. I could see it in her eyes, her need to try to resist. It's a need that I fully understand. Like her though, it's not something I can control.

For as much as I hate to admit that Hunter is right about anything, he is right about this.

Avery and I are meant to be.

"Hey, Mase," I hear Crystal's voice call out.

She's dressed completely inappropriately for a golf course. In fact, she's inappropriately dressed for really anywhere except a nightclub, maybe. But that's Crystal.

"I just wanted to go over a few things with you," she says when she reaches me.

"Good news or bad news?"

She gives me a big toothy smile, one that showcases her perfect teeth. "Thanks to Avery, good news. You better do whatever you can to keep that girl happy."

She pokes her finger into my chest.

"Ouch. I'm trying," I tell her.

"Try harder. Harder than you ever have for anything else because thanks to her – you are no longer looked at as some trouble making playboy."

"Really? It's only been a few weeks."

"Years, Mason. Years in the making. Best friends since you were kids? Now a blossoming, sexy romance? This is the stuff that romance novels are made of. And people are eating it up." Crystal takes a step closer to me and hands me a file folder.

Flipping through the contents, I stop on a photo of Avery and me from the event last week. This may all be a ruse, but that photo says otherwise. Even with her angry as hell at me, we still look good together. Happy even. Charade or not, this picture looks one thousand percent real. Like it's supposed to be.

"You two look good together," Crystal comments.

"Yeah, we do."

"Then don't be an idiot, Mase. Make whatever this is in this picture work. I have never seen you look happier than you have these past couple of weeks."

Just as Crystal presses a kiss to my cheek, Avery steps through the door. The entire moment is innocent, but it sure as hell doesn't look that way. Not to Avery, at least. I can see it in her eyes.

"Sorry to interrupt," she mumbles before turning to head out the door.

As much as I want to stop her, I don't know what to say.

Luckily for me, Crystal does. "Avery, I'm so glad you're here."

Avery stops and turns toward Crystal. "You are?"

"Of course." Crystal does that bubbly laugh of hers as she heads over to Avery. Taking Avery's hands in hers, she gives them a squeeze. "I was just telling Mason how well everything is going, and it's all thanks to you. His reputation is already on the rebound."

"That's great."

"I also told him, that you two are perfect together, and he better smarten up and make this thing real." Just like she had done to me, Crystal presses a kiss to Avery's cheek before skipping out the door. "Toodles."

Holding up the file in the air, I say, "She brought proof."

"Proof of what?"

Avery is still standing in the doorway. I nod my head, trying to coax her in. She slowly takes a step forward, then another, until she finally reaches me.

"How amazing we are together."

I hand the folder over to her.

She flips through it, then slams it shut. "All this proves is that they don't think I'm good enough for you."

"What are you talking about?"

"Didn't you read the comments on these?"

"No. I never do."

"Well, let me give you the CliffsNotes version. I'm too fat, not pretty enough, not…"

"Stop right there. First off, quit reading that shit. Second, that's exactly what it is… shit. Those comments are from women who are jealous of you, wishing they were in your shoes. You are amazing, Avery. Gorgeous, smart, funny. You're everything I could ever want in a woman."

"Except that you don't want a woman. Not for more than a night, at least. I get it."

She doesn't "get it." She can't. Because there is no way in hell she's going to believe what I'm about to tell her.

Years of me denying wanting anything more than sexual gratification, my continual denial about believing in love. No way in hell is she going to expect the curveball that I'm about to throw her.

The only problem is, for as much thought as I have given this, I never really planned what I wanted to say or how I wanted to tell her. Now that the moment's here, I freeze. I stare at her, completely affected and utterly lost. So, I do the only thing that I'm well versed in – the physical.

I pull her against me, my lips crashing onto hers. I pour the emotions that I can't express into this kiss; I pour everything into it and pray she feels it. Pray she understands what I don't know how to verbalize.

"Hey, one last thing," I can hear Crystal's voice. "Shit, sorry. Never mind."

Avery pushes me away, her hands pressing hard against my chest. "What is it, Crystal?"

"I just wanted to mention to Mason that he has a photo shoot tomorrow," Crystal says. "Don't be late."

Crystal mouths an apology to me as she backs out of the room.

The moment is ruined. I can already see Avery closing up again.

"We should go," she says softly.

No way in hell am I letting things go that easily.

"We have unfinished business that we need to take care of first," I tell her.

"What? That kiss?" She waves her hand in the air trying to make light of something we both know was unexpected and intense as hell. "It's fine. No big deal."

"It was more than fine." My hand reaches for her arm to stop her from walking away. "And it was definitely a big deal. So big that it scares the shit out of me, Ave. I... I know what it's like to not have you in my life now. And honestly? It fucking sucks. I am less than nothing without you."

"That's not true," she argues with me.

"There are very few things in the world that I'm certain of. One of them being you. You mean the world to me, Avery."

"You don't have to do this, Mason. I get it. It's fine."

"You don't get a damn thing, Avery, because you're not listening. I know I hurt you, and I'm sorrier than you will ever know about that. I assure you that us being together that night wasn't just about me staking a claim on you. It was about you. And that dress. And how much I fucking wanted you all night. Watching him with his hands on you – killed me. So yeah, I acted like a goddamn ass and pushed us into something we weren't ready for." I run my hands through my hair. "Something I wasn't ready for. I never meant to hurt you. I never meant to make you think that I used you or that you weren't enough. You are. You are so much better than what I deserve."

Her face softens, her eyes welling with tears.

"Forgive me, Ave. Because if you don't forgive me, we can't figure out what all this means. What we mean to each other. And I want to. Christ, I fucking want to."

"I can't, I'm sorry. I just... it hurts, too much." Avery pulls out of my arms and walks out the door. Once again, I watch her walk away when I should be running after her.

Chapter 23

Avery

I scroll down to the latest photo of us on the "Mave" FaceSpace page. Seriously, that's the name they came up with? The photo is amazing, and despite the several negative comments about me that follow, we look happy together. Like we're a couple. A real couple, not the one that we're pretending to be. It's that exact thought that sets off the butterflies in my belly.

It's been a week since the golf outing. A week since I lied to Mason and told him that I couldn't forgive him when the truth is, I already have. It's my feelings for him that I can't get past. The ones that confuse me and make me think of things that can't be. Will never be. Yet, every word, every touch, makes me believe them all the same.

No, I'm not mad at Mason anymore. I'm mad at myself for being a fool and falling for a man that is unattainable. It's like wishing for a unicorn when you know they don't exist.

"I thought I told you to quit looking at that shit," Mason's voice says from behind me. I had been so lost in thoughts of him that I hadn't even realized he was standing there.

Coach and Lou asked us to meet with them. I'm assuming it has something to do with our charade; I'm just not sure what. I would say it's because no one's buying the act, but I mean, we even have one of those disgusting couple names – what more do they want?

"I happen to like how I look in this picture, thank you very much," I say. There's a hint of humor in my voice.

Mason hasn't pushed or mentioned my inability to forgive him. We've just merely ignored the end of our last conversation as though it never even happened. He's being patient and sweet – everything he typically isn't. And every time that we speak, every time I give him a glimpse of the old us, he latches onto it. Like now.

Mason pulls up a chair and sits down next to me. He leans in close, too close for my comfort. "I like it, too. You look happy. I like seeing you happy."

"There they are," Lou boasts as he walks into the room. "Mave. The new "it" couple."

The sound of Lou uttering the word "Mave" has me rolling my eyes.

"How's everything going?" Coach asks. His eyes are locked on us, looking between Mason and me.

"You tell us," Mason deadpans. There's a reason we are here, and it's not so Lou can check up on us.

A moment later, Crystal walks in. I'm not surprised; she's the PR guru, after all. Still, I find myself feeling insecure immediately and adjust myself in my seat. And I hate that I hate her being here because, honestly, she seems genuinely nice. Yet, the fact that she was with Mason bugs the hell out of me. It makes me feel inferior to her and her perfection. She would have been a better match. She would have been more believable. She would be having sex with him during this little charade instead of continuously pushing him away like I am.

My conversation with Quinn early on, her telling me to show him what he's missing out on comes to mind.

I was going to give it a shot. A real shot, but I chickened out. Fear of his rejection, fear of my heart being broken overtook me, and instead, I built that damn wall to keep him out.

"I'm sure you're curious as to why we called you here," Crystal begins. Considering she was just praising our believability a few days ago, curious is an understatement. "Well, having scrolled through all the comments…"

The moment that I hear her say the word "comments," my body tenses. Here it comes, I don't fit the bill. We'll have to come up with another plan.

"The most mentioned thing is that you two don't spend enough time together," she concludes.

Relief washes over me when I hear the words. "That's it?"

"Were you expecting something else?" Crystal asks.

I shake my head. Of course, I was expecting something else. I was expecting me to be the problem. The woman who doesn't fit the bill. But there was no way in hell am I going to tell her that.

"What do you mean? We've been to every event, we go out once a week, we…."

"Sleep in separate beds. Don't ever spend the night at each other's places," Crystal adds in. "People expect you two to be inseparable. The way you were when you were "just friends." No offense, Mason, but this is you were talking about. And you two haven't spent more than five minutes alone."

"So, you want us to have sex?" Mason interjects. He shrugs. "Okay."

All the while, I'm just sitting here completely flabbergasted.

"The appearance that you are, yes. We just need you two to up your game," Crystal says as though it's the easiest thing in the world.

That's when it all finally registers. Sex. He told her we were going to have sex. "Mason," I scold him.

"I can kiss her more, too," Mason continues on. "Maybe walk with my hand on her ass?"

"This isn't funny," I say.

"I'm not joking," Mason replies.

I turn back to Crystal. "Is there anything else?"

The tension is rising between Mason and me, and it's more than obvious to everyone in the room. All I can think is to escape.

"Uh… no?" Crystal asks.

"Good," I reply as I push away from the table and exit the room.

"Avery, wait up," Mason shouts. He is hot on my heels. He sticks his arm between the closing elevator doors before jumping in with me.

I expect him to ask me what's wrong or why I left the meeting so abruptly. But none of that happens. Instead, a mischievous grin slides across his face. "Want to try that kissing thing?"

"I thought we were past that?"

"Who said that? You're a good kisser, and I fully intend on taking advantage of that."

"That's what got us into this mess in the first place," I retort, an extra bite to my tone.

"No, what got us into this mess was my big, stupid mouth and my fucked-up head." Mason presses the emergency button, the elevator jolting to a stop.

"What are you doing?" I ask, trying to reach around him.

With his hands on my arms, he backs me up against the elevator wall. "We're going to settle this once and for all."

"There isn't anything to settle."

"Like hell there isn't. Will you please quit being mad at me? Will you please help me figure out what the fuck I'm feeling and why I can't control it? I need you, Ave, in every fucking way imaginable."

"You don't mean that."

"I wish I didn't. You would be so much better off if I didn't. But I do. I mean every fucking word." That boyish grin of his graces his face. "Forgive me, Ave. I won't fuck up again."

The heat in his eyes is melting any resolve I have to not reach up and kiss him. I want him. I need him. Just as much as he says he wants and needs me. And when his lips brush against mine, I know he feels it, too. Somewhere deep inside him, the small space where he's not afraid to love or be loved, he feels this connection between us.

He pulls back, seeking permission for more. I don't grant him permission, though. I steal his thunder, his kiss, all of him. I take his face in my hands and allow him to consume me.

"Fucking hell," he groans into the kiss. The words almost inaudible. But I hear them, and I hear every single meaning behind them.

He wants this. He wants to stop this. He needs this. He sure as hell doesn't want to need this. Or me.

But it's inevitable. We are inevitable.

It's there, and it's real. This unspoken connection. This deep desire. A level of respect and comfort neither of us has ever been able to share with another soul. From the moment I first looked at him, I knew. I am his. When he wasn't mine. And now when he is.

He slowly ends the kiss, his forehead resting on mine. "I owe you better than this."

"What's better than sex in an elevator?" I tease him.

That's exactly where we were heading; there's no denying that.

"Christ, you really are made for me, aren't you? Just please don't ever tell me about that. The idea of you with anyone else… it kills me."

"Welcome to my world," I say. I begin to laugh, but the look in Mason's eyes halts that instantly.

Being in his arms only drives my need for a physical connection with him. For me, that's all that's missing. I always had the best parts of him; now I just need this. And to know that he feels it too.

The idea of protecting my heart flies right out the window, the need to be near him taking over. To hell with everything. To hell with the consequences.

It was the same thought I had that first night when he kissed me. Everything is different now. Now I know that he wants me. He may not want to, and he may not understand what he's feeling, but he's feeling it. Knowing that makes all the difference.

So, when his eyes implore me, questioning if I'm really okay with sex in an elevator, I drop my hands to the waistband of his jeans and unbutton them. "I need you, Mason."

I've always wanted him, that much I've known. It's so much more now. I need him. Every piece of him. The good, the bad, the sex. All of him. Broken, damaged, repaired.

When his hand slides under the skirt of my dress, his fingers make a beeline for my center. The growl he emits when he finds that I'm already soaked only increases the wetness.

"Now, Mason," I plead with him.

Any amount of hesitation he may have had dissipates into thin air. My hand frees him of the jeans he's donning at the same moment he tears away the small scrap of lace. Ready and waiting, I hold his face in my hands and lock eyes with him. The look we share, I hope expressing everything I need him to know. That I want this. That I want us. That no matter what, we're going to be okay because there is just no other option.

"Only you, Ave. Only you." He utters the words as he hoists me up. My legs wrap tightly around him, my lips meeting his.

Fire and Water.

Anger and forgiveness.

Hate and love.

This kiss embodies everything that we've ever felt as we realize for certain – we are the only people we've ever felt them for.

The moment he enters me, filling me and satisfying me the way that only he can, I sigh. A sense of completeness washes over me. Any wall I had pretended I constructed around my heart – demolished.

"Look at me, Ave."

My eyes flutter open, and I look at him. I look at him as he moves in and out of me. Each thrust a piece of his armor crumbling. Every kiss, a furthered understanding of what he feels. The physical he knows finally becoming an emotional entity he can wrap his head around. Not understand, he's not there yet, and that's okay.

A chance.

That's what this is giving us. A chance for him to accept and me to forgive, and us to explore whatever this is together.

Because isn't that how we always do things? Together.

Just the two of us?

With my body wedged between his and the elevator, he presses his hand against the wall as he drives into me, harder and faster, with an intensity I've never experienced before.

"Jesus, fuck," he cries out.

The sound of his voice, the way he's losing control – all because of me – sends me spiraling straight into my orgasm. I tighten and tremble, my body elated with the love and pleasure he's given me. His eyes never leave mine as he continues to move in me with a reckless abandon that has me crying out his name as he fills me one last time, one last powerful thrust. His head collapses onto my shoulder.

The position is impossible to stay in for long, so Mason sets me on the floor, but his eyes still don't leave me.

"What?" I ask, feeling almost shy under his intense gaze.

"You're it."

"I'm it? We playing a game of tag here, Mase?"

He finishes tucking himself back into his jeans and then takes a step toward me. "Yep, and I won." He cradles my face in his hands. "I'm going to figure out how to do this. I'm going to do right by you, Aves."

"I know you will," I tell him. My lips press against his in a chaste kiss that clearly isn't enough for him. As he deepens the kiss, branding himself and me, the doors to the elevator doors begin to open.

"You two okay?" Coach asks until he takes in the sight of us.

"Just fine," Mason replies. "Just fine."

Chapter 24

Mason

"So, does this mean that you forgive me?" I ask as we walk to her apartment door.

"Nope," she replies with a smile on her face. "I think you need to prove just how sorry you are a few more times."

"That's exactly what I had intended on doing. You're the one making me take you home."

When we finally left the stadium, I begged her to come home with me. There are a million things I want to do to her and a lot that we still need to talk about – figure out.

However, she has class at seven in the morning. A class that I know she's missed more than a few times due to events we've had to attend or just sheer and utter exhaustion.

I get it, and I can't ask her to make any more sacrifices for me than she already has.

"I'm sorry. You know how…"

"I'm only teasing you, baby."

When I call her baby, she comes to a dead stop. We both look at each other and burst out laughing. "That just doesn't sound right."

"It didn't sound right saying it either," I admit.

"I don't think we're going to be one of those cutesy pet name couples." No sooner does she say it, she freezes. I can see her body tense, the smile on her lips fading.

I don't think she regrets it; I think she's worried. Afraid that she's assumed incorrectly and that I might not want that.

"Sorry, I didn't mean that how it came out."

I cock my head to the side, "So, what, I'm just a booty call now?"

"What? No. I…" When she realizes that I'm just messing with her, she slaps my arm. "You're a jerk."

When we reach her door, I take her hand in mine. "I'm still trying to wrap my head around all of this," I admit.

I may know how I feel, but I'll be damned if I don't still understand it. Or fear it.

"I promise you though, I'm trying to figure it out. I just need your help. I need this to not be pretend anymore. I need it to be real."

"We've always been real."

"Then let's figure out, together, what we want this to be."

"I like the sound of that," she says as she tries to stifle a yawn.

"Time for you to get some sleep," I tell her.

"Talk more tomorrow?" she asks.

"If you think I am ever going another day without talking to you again, you're crazy."

Our lips meet, only briefly, before she pushes me away. "Don't forget, I know how you operate. And I need to get some sleep."

"Can't blame a guy for trying."

"Goodnight, Mason."

I steal one last quick kiss before turning and heading home.

******

I'm lost in thoughts of Avery and our time in the elevator that I almost don't notice the person in the shadows outside my condo. When I see who it is, I wish I hadn't.

The good mood Avery left me in quickly dissipates.

"What do you want?" I ask Trent.

"How do you do it?" He's leaning against the wall, a sinister look on his face.

"Do what?" I prompt him, trying to figure out what in the hell it is he's after. There has to be something. Some reason the guy hates me when up until a year ago, I didn't even have a clue who the fuck he was.

"How do you manage to get whatever you want without even having to try?"

"I don't know what the hell you're talking about."

"The team. Avery. Je…" He shakes his head. "Everything. You have everything."

"I worked for it, Trent. I busted my ass every day because I didn't have a choice. I didn't have anyone to take care of me or do anything for me. So, I did it. I did it for me. I did it for my sister. And fuck yes, I did it for Avery, too."

"You don't deserve it. None of it."

"Maybe not. But I got it because I worked for it. Why don't you get over your shit and do the same? Quit hating me and trying to destroy me and instead show us what you've got."

"You don't know a fucking thing about me," Trent shouts.

"And what is it that you think you know about me, huh? What is it that makes you hate me so damn much?"

Trent doesn't reply, only smiles. It's sinister and promising of trouble. Why? Why the fuck is he doing this?

"I will beat you, Ford. I will take everything you have and make it mine. Even Avery."

"I'd like to see you try," I challenge him.

"Game on."

Without a clue as to what fucking game we're playing, I watch him walk away. As much as I want to, warning him to stay away from Avery isn't going to do any good. I'll protect her myself, ensure that his unhinged ass never lays a finger on her.

"Hello?" her sweet voice says through the phone.

"Hey, I know you want to get to sleep, but… uh, I need to tell you something."

"What is it?" she asks, no beating around the bush. I can hear the worry in her voice, probably afraid I'm going to retract everything I said to her, the promises that I made.

"You need to be careful. When I got home, Trent was here and…" I wipe my hand down my face. "He is far from stable. I'm going to get you some security, but in the meantime, just…keep an eye out."

"Got it."

"This is not me overreacting, Ave."

It's the benefit of knowing each other so well; I know what she's thinking before she even has the opportunity to say it.

"I know. I just don't think he would do anything to hurt me. He's after your spot on the team, Mase. He's not going to do anything crazy to me."

That's the part that I'm not entirely sure about. Is it my spot he's after? Or is it just me? And doing something crazy? Isn't he kind of doing that already?

"Just be careful," I tell her.

"Always."

I don't want to hang up but know that I have to. "Goodnight... baby."

"Do not do that ever again." Her laughter fills the phone.

"Oh, come on, baby. Don't be like that, baby."

"Goodnight, Mason," she shouts over my ramblings.

Despite Trent showing up, that's what it was – a good night.

Chapter 25

Avery

Campus is quieter than usual tonight as I stroll through the grounds on my way to meet Mason.

I was surprised to receive the text from him asking me to meet him on campus tonight. Especially since it came in not long after we ended our phone call. I smile, wondering if he had been too nervous to ask. My smile grows, knowing that can't be possible, not after what we did in the elevator the other day. Not to mention the numerous things he told me he wanted to do to me afterward. My body shivers at the thought. God, how I want him to do those things to me.

I sit on the bench near the spot where we had our picnic weeks ago and glance down at my watch. I'm a few minutes early and know Mason well enough to know he'll be a few minutes late. My mind races as I sit here wondering what it is that he wanted to meet here of all places for.

"Hey, Avery," a familiar voice says. Just not the familiar voice I'm expecting to see.

"Trent," I exclaim, surprised by his presence. "What are you doing here?"

He stands tall, hovering over me with a smile on his face that has me questioning what his intentions are. Whatever they may be, I get the distinct impression that they aren't good.

Mason's warning seemed crazy when he gave it to me – beware of Trent. I had assumed that it was just that, a warning. A possessive, emotional warning. Now, I'm not so sure. Mason was right; Trent looks unhinged.

"I wanted to see you," he says.

"What do you mean you wanted to see me?" I ask.

It dawns on me that this was a set-up. Mason didn't text me. Trent did. He must have somehow gotten ahold of Mason's phone and sent the text.

Trent glances around the darkened campus. "It's a beautiful night, isn't it?"

"What do you want, Trent?" I ask.

"You."

"I'm with Mason."

"Are you really though?" he asks with a laugh. "Because I call bullshit. Mason Ford doesn't date. He takes what he wants no matter who he hurts in the process."

"That's not true."

"Isn't it? He took you from me, didn't he? He literally ripped you out of my arms and made you his."

I stare at him, unable to speak and not wanting to all the same. I'm afraid to set up off, to say something that could cause him to do... God knows what.

Trent looks on edge. Even more unstable than Mason had described. I slowly move my hand into my pocket, trying to reach for my phone. Just as I feel it, as I touch the screen, Trent grabs my arm and yanks the phone from my hand.

Shit.

"You know what your problem is?" he asks. "Mason. You should have picked me."

"You don't pick who you love," I tell him.

Trent laughs. "Love? You think Mason loves you?"

I know he does.

Trent's fingers reach out and touch my hair. "Mason doesn't know what love is. And now he never will."

I turn my head, the strand of hair he was holding falling from his hand. "You're not making any sense." My voice sounds eerily calm despite the fear that has taken over my very being.

"Sure I am. All I have to do to make him suffer is take away the one thing that matters to him. The one thing he thinks he loves."

Me.

Chapter 26

Mason

Quinn opens the door and looks at me with a confused smile. "What are you doing here?"

Returning her smile, I say, "I wanted to surprise Avery."

"Yeah, well, since you were supposed to meet her at campus ten minutes ago, I'm sure she'll be surprised."

"What are you talking about?"

Quinn shakes her head. Clearly, she thinks I've done something that I'm not aware of.

"Tell me," I demand.

"You're the one who texted her. You told her to meet you at campus at seven."

I reach for my phone and open my messages. There, clear as day, is a message telling Avery to meet me on campus. One that I very much did not send. I glance at the clock before looking back at the phone.

Fuck.

Without another word, I run out the door and head straight to campus.

I'm barely out of my car when I hear what sounds like a scream. Her scream.

"Avery," I shout as I run through campus at top speed.

The bench near where we had our picnic. That's what the text has said.

Christ, has he been following us? Watching us?

When I finally reach Avery, she's alone. There's no one else in sight, and all I can do is sigh in relief.

"Ave, you okay?"

"Go Mason, get out of here," she says.

"I'm not leaving without you." I take a step toward her, and she begins to shout.

"Stop. Don't come any closer."

"Why not? Ave, tell me what's going on?"

There's a loud sound, similar to a firework being set off.

"No," Avery's voice screams as I watch her charge toward me.

What in the fuck is she doing?

In a flash, she's in my arms, a gut-wrenching cry escaping her. Her body is limp, falling against mine.

"Avery," I cry as I ease her onto the ground. "Why the fuck would you do that?"

"Because I love you."

Her eyes close as I fumble for my phone to call the police.

"I'm sorry, Mason."

The sirens get closer as I hold onto her, pleading with her to hold on, to be okay.

"I love you, too. Okay? You can't do this. You can't leave me."

The paramedics arrive, moving me out of the way. The police bombarding me with questions that I don't have the answers to. At least not real answers. I have my assumptions. I know deep down who did this.

I sure as hell don't need the police to help me make him pay.

******

He's going to pay for this.

It's the sole thought running through my head as I sit at her bedside, her hand in mine.

She's asleep, has been since they brought her in, since she told me she's sorry, and I have no idea what it is that she's sorry for. Christ, she isn't the one that should be sorry about anything. It's me.

"I'm sorry, Ave. I'm sorry I fucked everything up, I'm sorry I let you get caught in the middle of whatever this shit show is."

I rest my forehead against her hand and squeeze my eyes shut. The memory of her running toward me. The feel of her body hitting mine. The words "I love you" falling from her lips.

Any doubt that I may have had left was gone the moment I saw her standing there. Me. Her. My feelings. What once felt completely out of my depth now felt undeniably understandable. I run my hands through my hair, not even sure if the thoughts running through my head make any sense.

All I know is that everything I've been trying so desperately to deny, to run from, smacked me right in the face.

Avery and I, we are more than just friends. More than just family. We are soul mates.

Emotions that I never wanted to feel, things I didn't understand, suddenly make sense and exist solely for her.

As she stared at me, as the bullet hit her, her eyes were filled with love. Her words solidifying what her eyes already told me. So much damn love that it literally took my breath away. And I haven't been able to recover since. I'm not even sure if I want to.

"Mase?" The sound of Quinn's voice behind me eases the ache slightly. The three of us, a family, at least were all still together. Even if one of us is currently in a deep sleep.

"She's going to be okay," I tell Quinn. It's not her I'm trying to convince though. It's me.

"Of course, she is," Quinn replies, her hand resting on my shoulder. "There is no way in hell she would leave you to your own devices."

"Especially not after what happened last time," I chime in. The recollection of just how badly I fell apart when she walked out of my life for being an asshole hits me. It's nothing compared to how I would be if she actually were to leave me for good – the kind of gone with no possibility of return.

"That's right. She also wouldn't want you sitting here, just waiting. She would want you to go and get some rest," Quinn says.

Funny thing is, I can actually hear Avery's voice agreeing with her, arguing with me that I'm not doing either of us any good sitting here just staring at her. She would be wrong, though. Sitting here, staring at her, it's the only thing keeping me sane. Her face, soft and sweet and seemingly pain free, is holding me together.

"I'm rested enough."

"Mason…"

"Drop it, Q. I'm not going anywhere."

I hear the sound of a chair scraping across the floor, and moments later, Quinn is sitting next to me. "Then I'll join you."

"We were doing perfectly fine on our own."

"Hey, she's my family, too."

I glance at Quinn, who is sitting next to me, trying to hold it together while she secretly wants to fall apart.

Family.

I wrap my arm around her and pull her close, pressing my lips to her temple. "She's going to be okay."

Quinn's head rests against my shoulder as we sit side by side in the uncomfortable hospital chairs. At some point, we must have both dozed off, the stress and worry taking over. Because the next thing I know, a familiar voice is speaking, and my hand is being squeezed.

"Mason, wake up," Avery says. Her voice is scratchy and soft as she speaks. The moment I hear her voice, my eyes pop open, and my body jolts, startling Quinn awake.

"Avery? You're awake," I say, my hands running over her hair as I press my lips to her forehead.

"What happened? Where am I?"

"Quinn, go get the doctor," I tell her. She rushes out of the room.

"There was an accident," I say, though I am not sure that's the most accurate description.

Attack? Maybe. Sabotage? Definitely.

The people who did this to her clearly were trying to get to me. In the least, affect me and throw me off my game. Whatever it takes to make Trent look like the better player and me… not.

"You're going to be okay, though. Everything is," I say. My words are a promise. A realization. One that, as soon as she's better, I fully intend on sharing with her.

Seeing what they did to her. The idea of losing her, really losing her, it made me realize what all of this meant. What these feelings, I was sure, were nothing more than friendship really were. They're love. And not the sisterly kind of love I feel for Quinn. The forever kind of love that I can only feel for Avery.

The doctor comes in a few minutes later and ushers Quinn and me out of the room so he can examine her.

"You okay?" Quinn asks as she watches me pace the hallway.

"Yeah. I'm good. I'm…" I stop in my tracks, then turn to face her. "I love her, Quinn. You were right. This thing between us is so much more than I ever gave it credit for."

"About damn time," she says with a smile.

"Give me a break, okay? I might be a little slow on the uptake, but… I got here, and there is no way in hell am I letting her go now."

After the doctor clears Avery, the police arrive to take her statement. I did my best to keep them away, but she wanted to talk to them to tell them who did this to her.

Standing off to the side, I lean against the wall while the officer begins to ask her questions. "What were you doing on campus at that hour?"

"I had received a text from Mason to meet him there," she replies.

The officer glances over at me, then back to her. "And did he show?"

She shakes her head. "No. He uh, he's not the one that sent the text. The person that showed up was Trent. Trent Roth."

"What?" I shout, pushing away from the wall and next to her bed.

"Mason, calm down," she says.

All the other possibilities of things he could have done to her are racing through my mind. "I am not going to calm down. No, what I'm going to do is fucking kill him," I say. The officer next to me clears his throat to remind me of his presence and the very clear-cut threat I made. "Did he touch? Did he…"

"No. No. Nothing like that, Mase. I swear." She takes my hand in hers and squeezes it, but it does little to help calm me. Nothing except tearing that son-of-a-bitch to pieces is going to help.

"Mr. Roth showed up, then what happened?"

Avery continues to recant her conversation with Trent. The one that ended abruptly when I arrived unexpectedly.

"Did you actually see him shoot the gun?" the other officer asks.

"No. It was too dark to see. But he was the only one there."

"Is there anything else you can remember from that night?"

"No, not that I can think of."

"I think we're done here, officer," Lou says, stepping into the room. "You can contact our attorney if you have any more questions."

The officers shake their heads and Lou's abrupt interruption. He stands in the doorway, holding it open for them. The moment they exit, he locks the door behind them.

"What you two need to do is keep your damn mouths shut. Be in love, be happy. Be grateful you're both okay from this horrific accident."

"But..." I begin to argue.

"No but's on this, Mason."

The look on Lou's face worries me, so I agree. The only thing that matters now is keeping Avery safe.

Chapter 27

Avery

"Will you at least go home and shower? You're starting to smell," Avery teases; the smile on her face is infectious.

"I'm not going anywhere unless I get to take you home with me," I reply.

Home with him? He's not suggesting what I think he is. Is he?

I'm not going to complain about the idea, but I have to admit with everything between us still kind of unsettled and up in the air, I don't feel like it's the best idea. I think, for Mason's sake, we need to take things slow. Figure them out.

"Mason..."

"No arguments Avery. You're staying with me. I need to know you're safe."

"I wasn't the intended target," I remind him. His safety much more on the line than my own. The bullet was heading toward Mason. Not me. I just did the only thing I could think of when I saw what was happening. I protected him.

The nurse walks in, a pleased smile on her face. "Somebody's getting sprung from his joint."

"Looks like we both get our way," Mason says.

"How so?" I ask.

"I get to go home, and take a shower and you get to come with me." He leans in, his voice dropping to a whisper. "I might even let you shower with me if you're nice."

"You certainly do know how to bribe a girl."

"So, that's a yes?"

"It's a yes."

"Good. I already had Quinn bring your things to my place." Smug jerk.

"You're pretty sure of yourself, aren't you?" I say with a laugh.

"When it comes to getting women to do what I want? Yeah, I am."

I let out a sigh and roll my eyes at him. "Whatever you say, stud. Let's go home."

******

When we step into his condo, I'm surprised at how much like home it does feel. Though, I do suppose we've spent so much time here that it should. Mason bought this place the moment he signed with the Red Devils. He was so excited. A real place – all his own. The first night, we all stayed here. Me, him, Hunter, even Quinn. Granted, back then, she and Hunter fought like dogs. Even still, it was a nice night.

Then there was the shopping. The condo was expansive, with way too much space for one person. Especially when that person had basically been living in closet sized spaces most of their lives. Mason and I spent hours looking at furniture and little touches. Anything to make this place look like a home rather than just some bachelor pad.

"Are you okay?" he asks.

"Aside from this massive headache? Yeah, I'm great."

"Why don't you lie down for a while," he suggests. "The uh, the guest room is all ready for you."

I'm grateful but slightly surprised he said guest room. Knowing Mason, I assumed he was going to keep both eyes on me as long as he could. Still, a couple rounds of sex and some confused emotions does not lend itself to being a relationship. Certainly not one that should be taken to that sort of level. The room sharing kind.

He pushes the door to the room open. He wasn't kidding when he said it had been prepared for me. I can smell the fresh paint and see the fresh linens.

My hand flies to my chest. "Mason, it's beautiful. You didn't have to go to all this trouble."

"It wasn't any trouble. Besides, after getting you into this mess, it was the least that I could do." I hear him grumble the word "literally" under his breath.

"Don't do that, Mase. None of this is your fault."

"I dragged you into this."

"You didn't drag me into anything," she argues. "I walked into it. And into that bullet. And I would do it again in a heartbeat."

"I'm not sure that makes it any better."

"When are you going to stop blaming yourself?" Sitting down on the bed, exhaustion overcoming me, I stare at him, willing him to answer the question.

"I'll go so you can get some rest."

"Answer the question, Mason. When are you going to quit thinking that everything that goes wrong is your fault? When are you going to quit thinking that you're him? When are you going to realize that everything good that's ever happened to me is because of you? Not the bad. The good, Mase."

"You were shot," he shouts, his hand hitting his chest. "Because of me. And I couldn't protect you. I couldn't help you."

"I was shot because Trent is psychotic. I was shot because he shot me, Mason. Not you. Whatever is going on in his sick, twisted mind is on him. Not you."

"I hurt you, Ave."

"Did you not hear what I just said?"

He shakes his head. "I hurt you. I broke your heart and your trust. I did that. Not Trent. Not a gun. Me."

"Oh, Mason."

"How can I give you more than my friendship when I can't even manage the one thing I swore to you I would do."

My eyes are on him, never blinking. Never drifting away. I'm studying him. Trying to figure out what in the hell it is that he's talking about. "What one thing?"

"When I asked you to leave home, to come with me to the city, I promised you that I would be the one person in your life who never hurt you. I failed you."

Rushing as quickly as my still weakened body will allow, I go to him. I force him to look at me and see the emotion that I have for him. The love. Love that never disappeared no matter what we have gone through. A heart that never in a million years could stop loving him or think that he failed me.

"You have never failed me," I assure him. "You have been everything to me. You pick me up when I'm down. You make every piece of my life better."

"Except when I didn't."

"That wasn't all on you, Mase. It was on me, too. And I'm sorry. I'm sorry if I took my broken heart out on you. Your words, yes, they hurt me. The idea that you would use me to get back at some guy that didn't matter, it hurt, too. But I forgave you. Long before I let you know I did. I…" It's me that turns away now. Guilt eating away at me. "I left because you hurt me, but I stayed away because of me. I thought if I stayed away, if I stayed mad at you, it would be easier. That somehow, my heart would miraculously stop loving you and wanting you."

"Did it?" he asks.

I walk over to the window and stare into the night. "Not even a little."

Mason comes up behind me. His body pressing against mine, hands clasped and resting on my stomach.

"I never want to be that guy again. The guy that hurts you. The guy that makes you want to walk away. I just don't know how to do that yet. Or if I even can."

"That's okay, Mase. There's no rush. I'm not going anywhere. You're stuck with me."

He presses a kiss to the top of my head. "I've never heard anything better."

We stay exactly like this for what feels like forever. Exhaustion be damned, I will stay like this forever. His arms are the only place I want to be.

Trying to deny my heart was impossible.

Not loving him – improbable.

Chapter 28

Avery

The blindfold falls away, my eyes adjusting to the street lighting. Glancing around me, I take in the familiar scenery before turning my gaze to the man who brought me here.

"What's this?" I ask Mason, who is standing behind me, his foot nervously kicking the ground.

We are at the park. The park that is nestled in the neighborhood we grew up in. It's the park we spent many days and nights in, including our prom night. Everything looks just as I remember it. A little more dated, sure, but the playground, the benches, they're all exactly where I remember them being.

"Why did you bring me here?"

I ask the question, but he doesn't respond. He just stares at the ground.

"Mason," I say. His name a demand that falls from my lips.

"I'm an asshole on a good day," Mason says. His head is still down, but his eyes raise to meet mine for a second. "On a bad day, I'm an asshole who hurts one of the few people that I actually care about." He raises his head, his eyes meeting mine dead on. "The thing is what you heard me tell Hunter – it's true. I took you home that night to prove that you were mine. To claim you like some fucking Neanderthal. None of it had to do with Trent, though. It had to do with you and that dress and all these damn things you made me feel that I didn't understand.

They're things that I still don't understand. Things I'm terrified of."

"Like what?" I ask softly, feeling like I need to interject something here but also not wanting to scare him off when I know just how hard this is for him. Emotions and feelings are not his strong suit. They aren't something he likes feeling, let alone discussing.

"Wanting you. Needing you. Losing you." He hangs his head. "I guess I already lost you, but…"

Taking a step closer to him, I take his face in my hands. "You haven't lost me, Mase. I'm right here."

"Are you though? Or is you being here just a part of this act?" he asks.

Lights flicker on, soft music begins to play.

"Because this isn't an act to me. Not anymore," he says. "Hell, I'm not sure it ever was."

"I don't understand," I reply as I look at the park transformation he made. The one that is telling of how well he knows me, how much we matter to him.

"Neither do I." It's an honest answer. Not exactly the one I had been hoping for, but the truth behind it, the emotion behind it, is undeniable. "You were my best friend, my rock, for my entire life. Every damn bit of strength I have comes from wanting to protect you. It was always you. Not one single woman I've ever been with could hold a candle to you even on your worst day. It took me a long time, too long, to realize what all of this meant. What it is that you mean to me."

"What do I mean to you?" I ask hesitantly, afraid to hear the answer.

"Everything," he deadpans. "And you know what?"

"Not a clue."

"It scares the shit out of me. Fuck, Avery, those few weeks without you, they broke me. The world stopped spinning – or at least mine did. You, Avery, you're my sunrise, my sunset, and everything in between. I know I fucked up. I know I made a huge ass mess of, well, everything. Let me fix it. Let me make this up to you. Show you that... I can be the guy you think I am. You deserve the world, Avery. I want to be the guy to give it to you."

My hand presses against my chest desperately, trying to tame the rapid beating. "Mason... I...."

"You don't have to say anything. I just needed you to know how I felt. How sorry I am. That there was so much more to me taking you home that night than to just stick it to Trent. It was me needing you – wanting you. It was me not understanding the depths of what I was feeling but feeling it all the same. You're mine, Avery. I want you to be mine."

His words are all over the place. His emotions strewn haphazardly all over his sleeve. While most wouldn't understand, I do. Where someone would question his intentions or his words, I don't. This, right here, this makes sense. The man who used me? He doesn't exist. He was just a very confused portion of the man standing before me. A version of himself that was too scared to accept what he was feeling.

To most, I'm sure it would sound like I'm making excuses. To anyone who knows us – they know. They know that this is us, and the level of our understanding of each other is far deeper than either of us can explain.

Inevitable.

It's what we are. It's what we always will be.

"If you think I don't have anything to say… then you've been hit in the head with a football one too many times," I tell him. "I'm yours, Mason. I have always been yours. I always will be."

His lips meet mine, tender and sweet. Emotions that are so foreign to him are pouring out of this kiss. Every word left unspoken; every promise left unsaid – we're saying it now.

When he pulls back, when he looks at me, tells me that he's going to fuck this up, I tell him I know. "I'll be right here helping you fix it."

Knowing how he feels, the certainty his words have provided me dispel every fear. Mason Ford doesn't wear his heart on his sleeve. He doesn't tell you what's in his heart. But he told me. And that alone tells me all I need to know.

This is real. We are real.

That is all I need to make this work. To fight.

"It's what we do, Mase," I continue on. "We balance each other out. When I need you, you've got my back. And when you need me…"

"I always need you."

"Then I'll be right here. Always."

Another kiss. His lips against mine sealing this undeniable and unexpected union.

"This is way better than prom night," I say with a soft laugh.

Taking my hand in his, he leads me to the bench. The very one that we sat on that night all those years ago. "I thought about kissing you that night," he admits.

"I wish you would have," I say in return.

"How long have you... why didn't you ever..."

I give him a slight peck on the cheek. "It feels like forever. And I never said anything because I just wanted you in my life. If that meant only being your friend, I was okay with that."

"You are a much better person than I am," he laughs, passing me the bottle of tequila that he just took a swig from. "You know, I have no clue how this whole relationship thing works."

"Believe me, I know," I tease.

He bumps his shoulder against mine, making me spit out some of the tequila I had not yet swallowed.

"Hey," I scold him. "What I meant was...I know you think you have no clue, but honestly, we've been doing it our whole lives."

There's a confused look on his face. His brown eyes rolling hard at my comment.

"It's true," I tell him. "A relationship is nothing more than two people who like to be together. Two people who share an emotional connection. Two people who..."

"Fuck a lot?" He raises his eyebrow in question.

"I was going to say, have each other's backs, but yes, that too."

"So? How do I rate in the boyfriend category?"

"I'll need to try another round of that fucking thing to say for sure, but other than that.... Five stars."

"We can most definitely rectify that right now."

"Right here?"

A wickedness flashes through his eyes right before he kisses me. This time his kiss is hard and fast. "Christ, I need you."

The groan reverberating from the back of his throat is filled with sexual tension and dripping with hunger.

"Take me, Mason. Make me yours. For real this time."

He pulls me onto his lap. "You're a naughty girl, aren't you?"

"Let's find out," I say as I hike up the hem of my skirt.

He runs his finger along the lace of my panties. The pure heat his touch surges through me makes me gasp. My hands grip his shoulders. It's all I can do to now force my body down onto his fingers. I've wanted this for too long. Needed him for longer.

"Please, Mason," I beg.

His voice is deep and husky in my ear, "Say it again."

"Please, Mason. Please, fuck me."

This time, he doesn't even try to hide the growl he emits. It's deep and primitive, and it sends a jolt straight to my core.

"Undo my pants." His words are a direct order, one that I am eager to comply with. He isn't making the task easy for me as his fingers trace over the lace before tugging them to the side. His finger slides into me with ease, my center dripping wet for him and only him. His thumb rubs my clit in lazy circles. All the while, my hands shake, and my body spasms under his touch. He teases me until I lose control, my body sinking down onto his finger, then rising again and repeating the motion.

"That's it, baby," he coos, his voice gruff.

Finally, after what feels like an eternity of fumbling and struggling, I manage to undo his button and zipper enough to slip my hand inside and grab what I want.

"Oh, fuck," he cries out the moment my skin connects with his. The hiss, the moan, every sound he makes encouraging me to be that naughty girl he thinks I am.

His finger slides out of me, and he brings it to his lips. "So good."

"Now, Mase."

With his cock free and my pussy soaked, we collide together in a fit of passion. He holds my hips as though he's hanging on for dear life, his eyes locked on mine as I ride him fast and hard. His hips buck up, his cock hitting me deep, making me scream out his name.

"Easy there," he says, his hand covering my mouth. "We are in public after all."

I'm amazed I had forgotten that little fact. So, lost in him that I had forgotten the world around us. How is that possible? How have I gone all these years without him like this?

We keep the unrelenting pace, each chasing something completely different yet very much the same. A satisfaction that is based solely on pleasing the other person – make each other ours.

Chapter 29

Mason

With Avery still nestled on my lap, my very pleased, very exhausted dick lies on my stomach. The occasional twitch telling me he isn't done with her yet. Not that I need that reminder. Because I sure as hell am not done with her either.

The first time Avery and I had sex was amazing. So much better than anything I experienced before. But this? Right now? Out of this goddamn world.

"Stay with me tonight," I tell her.

The last thing I want to do is leave this spot, but I know that we can't stay here all night. I refuse to be without her, though. Another first for me. Yet, with it being Avery, it's not completely. She's the only woman I've ever spent the night with, usually curled up on the couch passed out from watching a movie, or hell, even drinking too much. Tonight though, I want her in my bed. In my arms. I want to experience that with her – only her.

I want her to be my first – and my last.

"Are you sure?"

My lips press against the exposed skin above her breast. "I don't want to let you go, Ave. Not tonight. Not ever." I look up at her, my eyes heavy and in need of sleep. "I want you to move in with me. Really move in. In my room. My bed. For real. None of this pretend shit."

"Mason," she gasps. "It's pretty…"

"Sudden? Believe me, I know. I just… it feels right."

She worries her bottom lip between her teeth. "Mase, you've never even dated someone before. Don't you think maybe you should get used to that before we start living together?"

"I've been dating you my whole life, Ave. I just never realized it."

"Well, if that's the case. We need to have a long talk about all those other women…"

"What women?" I ask. "From the moment your lips met mine, no other woman existed."

"Smooth," she says as she presses her lips against my neck. "You keep talking like that, and I might just move in with you."

"You're the only woman for me. I want you by my side all the time."

She tosses her head back and laughs. I don't. I remain honest and focused, my eyes trained on her, waiting for her gaze to meet them.

When she does, her mouth falls open. "You really mean this, don't you?"

"More than anything." I pause for a moment. The words I'm about to say, words I have never spoken to a soul outside of a quick "love ya" to Quinn. "I love you, Avery. I love you, and I want you by my side."

As I speak, I can see the tears welling in her eyes. Unsure of what I've done, what I could have said to make her cry when I thought my words would bring her joy, I begin to panic eternally. I try to take back and proclaim the words again, all at one time. "I'm sorry. I didn't mean to blurt that out. If I upset you…"

"Upset me?" she laughs. Her hand caresses my cheek. "You didn't upset me, Mase. You made me happy. The happiest I have ever been."

While I know we're a far cry from perfect, mostly me, I also know that we're together, and that's what counts. No matter what, I believe that she's better off without me, that I'm just like him; whatever fear I let play me, I won't let it destroy us. Maybe those things are true. Maybe they're not. I can only be one hundred percent certain of one thing. My life, without Avery, is meaningless. That means I will do whatever it takes to keep her in it.

Chapter 30

Mason

Happiness.

Who would have ever thought it was for a guy like me?

Not me, that's for sure.

Maybe it's a bit of an exaggeration. It's not like I was completely unhappy before. I am a defensive end for my favorite team in the NFL. It was my dream come true. What isn't there to be happy about? Still, I always felt like something was missing. Even more when Avery walked out of my life.

Now, the piece of the puzzle is no longer missing. Everything feels complete. Me and Avery together – it's the happiest I have ever been. I'm at peace for what feels like the first time in my life.

"Hey, Mase," her voice says from the doorway to the kitchen.

The island in the kitchen is set with a buffet of food.

"Morning, gorgeous. You hungry?" I ask her.

A smile plays on her lips. Lips that taste so fucking sweet, I couldn't stop kissing them last night. Her smile is infectious, making me crack a smile of my own as I stand here staring at her and thinking about last night. My naughty girl in the park. The over-the-top sex when we got back here. The way she felt in my arms as I held her tightly all night. It wasn't the most comfortable thing, and for a moment, I admit, it felt pretty damn weird. As I continued to hold her, as my arms held on just a little tighter out of necessity, a level of tranquility settled over me. Soon my eyes became heavy, the awkwardness turned to comfort, and the smell of her shampoo is the last thing I remember thinking about.

"All this is for me?" she asks as she saunters in my direction.

"Yep. You worked hard last night. Thought you might have worked up quite the appetite."

"Oh, I did."

Her hands, however, don't reach for the plethora of food. They reach for me, for the elastic band of the shorts I'm wearing. She tugs on them, pulling me closer to her. Teeth nip at my neck while her hands work their magic inside my red shorts. She slides her body down mine, sinking to her knees. The moment she hits the floor, she takes me in the perfect 'O' her lips have made. I pull her hair back, my hand fisting the strawberry blonde strands so I can watch as she works me, sucks me, turns me into a fucking mess. Warm, wet, perfection.

My eyes are glued to her, watching every sexy damn motion. Aside from how good she feels, the determined and pleased look on her face nearly has me coming. I ease her off me. As I look down at her, mouth agape, eyes wide, I fall even more in love with her. Even more in lust, too, because the sight undoes me. I hoist her up and set her on the counter, sweeping the food off it because there is only one thing I want to feast on. Her.

The dishes hit the floor with a crash, the sound of glass shattering around us. None of it phasing me or based on the intensity in her eyes, her either. My hand moves to her throat, pulling her to me, taking those lips and intertwining our tongues.

When I end the kiss, when I press her onto the counter, I leave my hand in place as I lower my head to her center. One swipe of my tongue down her glorious seam, the slightest sucking of her swollen clit, and her hips are bucking off the counter, begging for more.

Christ, I love it when she begs.

I'm loving even more being able to give her what is it that she's craving. Me.

I taste, I tease, and I taunt her until she's gasping for more. Her hands grab mine, the one settled on pinning her down against the counter. Fear that I have pushed too far settles over me, and I immediately begin to retract my hand, but she stops me. She forces it down more, a strangled whimper escaping her.

"Fuck," I shout, after taking one last taste of her.

I pull her to the edge, let her control the pressure I apply to her delicate, delicious neck, and I press into her. No ease, no tenderness, I press into her fully, deeply, and I curse loudly. She moves with me, her hips meeting me thrust for thrust. Utter pleasure washes over me as I lose myself in us. No thoughts, no worries, nothing but how amazing this moment feels. How amazing she feels.

And when that feeling becomes overwhelming, and she tightens around me, we both tumble over the edge.

"Holy shit, Ave," I say as I rest my head on her stomach.

"That was…."

"Yeah, it was."

She props herself up on her elbows, her fingers lacing through my hair. "I'm starving."

I glance up at her, then down to the floor. "Looks like we're going out to breakfast," I say with a laugh. "You know what that means."

"Uh… no. What?"

"Time to hit the showers, baby," I say.

A quick wink before my arms encircle her, tossing her over my shoulder.

The squeal of delight, like music to my ears. A gentle reminder of what I've been missing all my life and how much time I've wasted. I'm fully intent on making it up for that now.

******

Laughter. The sound of it drowns out the rest of the world. We're sitting in the restaurant, all eyes on us, I'm sure. Not just because of me. Because of her. Her laugh – loud, happy, and most of all genuine. I'm not sure if the onlookers can see the difference between us, but God knows I can. She seems lighter, freer, and me? I feel like a whole new man. One that is experiencing a new and exciting world for the first time.

While so much of this feels familiar, so much of it feels new and exciting, too. This right here, it's how we used to be. Happy and laughing. Before I fucked everything up. But now, there's more. And maybe it's a little happier, a little extra. And I love it.

"You have practice later today?" she asks me.

"About that…" I begin.

I was supposed to go back to practice today. After everything with Avery and the shooting, I took a week off. The call I received from Coach this morning instructed me to take an extra day. Seems that Trent was coming in to meet with management to discuss his current "situation," and Coach thought it would be best if I just laid low.

"So, it looks like I'm all yours today," I tell her.

"Mase, I am so sorry," she tells me as she gives my hand a squeeze.

"You have nothing to be sorry for." My lips press against the soft skin at the back of her hand. "I am more than happy to have this time with you."

That isn't some bullshit line either. After everything, it's been amazing to have this time to really let ourselves just be and explore this new territory. Well, new territory for me, but still. It's exciting and new, and for as well as I know Avery, I feel like I'm getting to know her all over again. It's like seeing her but through a clearer lens.

"We can start moving stuff. Or redecorating. Or…"

"Slow down. There is no need to start redecorating." Another laugh. Another beat of my heart.

"I want you to be comfortable."

Her hand rests on top of mine. "I am comfortable. I've always been comfortable at your place."

"Our place," I correct her. That's what I want it to be. That's what I want it to feel like to her.

"Our place," she repeats.

I know that despite everything we've shared, everything we've been through together, the idea of "our" and "us" is still new and foreign for both of us. It's also right. So, damn, right.

"Well, I guess there is one thing." She looks down at her hands as she says the words.

"Name it."

"You could use a new comforter."

"What's wrong with my comforter?" I ask.

She tosses her head back in laughter. "You really need to ask that question?"

I ponder her words for a moment. Luckily, she pulls me out of my misery. "The sheer number of women who have touched those sheets." She shudders. "Probably should just get a whole new bed altogether."

Oh, Christ.

"If it gets you in it sooner, I will buy whatever the fuck you want."

Chapter 31

Avery

Realization strikes as I walk into Mason's condo. Our condo. This is real. This isn't part of the charade to make him look like a stand-up guy. This is real.

I drop my bag on the chair next to the door. Mason won't be home for another hour which gives me plenty of time to cook us dinner so we can actually spend some time together. As perfectly as everything is going, we've also both been insanely busy. The Red Devils are riding high, and as long as they keep it up, they're most definitely headed to the Super Bowl. And I'm finishing up my semester and trying to study for exams and work on my thesis.

Some days it feels like we are ships passing in the night.

Other days, God himself couldn't separate us.

For as long as we've known each other, as well as we know each other, admittedly, I was fearful that the transition from friendship to romance would be awkward. Take time even, especially with me having to move in after the attack. Surprisingly, the whole thing has been easy. Seamless even.

I stroll into the kitchen, evidence that I was beaten to the punch laid out on the island. I stand in the doorway, my arm resting against the wall as I watch him try to figure out what he's doing. The man can grill ten pounds of chicken like no one's business. But whatever he's attempting to make has him cursing at the iPad set out on the counter.

"How the fuck do you do that?" he yells at the screen.

I stifle the giggle that threatens to escape. Watching him, seeing him like this, it warms my heart. Such a far cry from the man he is so terrified of becoming.

I watch him struggle for a few moments longer, making sure to memorize this gentle, vulnerable side of him.

"Need some help?" I ask.

"Avery," he exclaims as he whirls toward me. "You're early."

"I am," I say with a nod. "I wanted to surprise you."

His eyes dart around the room, examining the mess he's made. "Same?"

"Oh, believe me, I'm surprised at what a mess you made," I tease him.

"Cute." Mason takes a step toward me.

"Yes, you are."

"Nice try." He lunges for me, grabbing me around the waist and pulling me against him. The mess of the kitchen that was strewn all over him pressing all over me now.

"Stop," I squeal as he makes sure to do his best to coat me in whatever it is that he has all over him.

"Quit picking on me."

"Never," I laugh.

This isn't the first time we've played this game. Though, it is the first time it was because he was cooking dinner. Where before, we would pull apart and just laugh, this time, he pulls me in for a kiss before finally releasing me.

"I tried," he concedes. "But I think we're going to have to order in."

"What were you trying to make?" I ask, surveying the kitchen. There is flour everywhere. Spaghetti sauce splattered on the counter. A stack of vegetables sits in the corner. And chocolate chips are everywhere.

"Lasagna?" he phrases the statement as a question as though even he's unsure of what he's trying to make.

"Chocolate lasagna?" I ask as I pop a morsel into my mouth.

"Shit," he exclaims. He pulls open the oven door, and smoke billows out. His head falls back, and another expletive falls from his lips. "They were supposed to be chocolate chip cookies."

Waving my hand around to clear the smoke, I bend to look into the oven. The tray with what was supposed to be cookies looks more like little black mountains.

"I love chocolate chip cookies."

"I know." He sounds defeated and sexy as hell.

I step up to him, my lips pressing to his neck. "I love it. All of it."

"It's a disaster."

"It is, but it's the sweetest disaster I have ever seen," I tell him. I mean every word because no one has ever taken the time to do something like this for me. Not even something this disastrous.

"Yeah, well, I promise I am much better at things I can buy. Like a car. I could buy you a car."

"I know, but I don't need a car. I don't need anything except some dinner and some time to just... talk to you."

It really has been a long week, a busy week where we didn't get to see each other very often. "I have been looking forward to just that all day."

"Then I'll order dinner, we'll eat it on the couch, and I will rub these gorgeous shoulders of yours. How's that?"

"Perfect. Except for one thing. I really want to make lasagna now. How about I finish dinner, you shower, and pick out a movie for us."

"You know we're not going to actually watch the movie, right?"

"I'm counting on it, actually."

******

An hour later, we are sitting on the floor in the living room, our plates of lasagna before us and a bottle of wine on the table.

"There's something I need to tell you."

"That doesn't sound good," Mason says, moving closer to me.

"It's not bad; it's just..."

"Spit it out, Avery."

"I took a job in New York. When I graduate, when the year is up, I'm supposed to move there."

Mason's face falls. The blissful state we were in only moments ago, gone.

"Is that what you want?" he asks.

I'm surprised by the question. I had expected an argument, a demand not to leave, but not a question. Not him asking what it is that I want.

"I want the job, yes. And I accepted it because, well, I thought putting distance between us might help. I wanted to get as far away from you as I could."

"Still want to?"

I shake my head. "No. But, I don't know what I'm going to do about a job. Or money. Or really anything."

Mason reaches for the bottle and refills my glass. "Lucky for you, you have me. You don't' have to worry about anything, Aves. I have your back."

"I know you do, and I love you for it, but…"

"No buts. You help me with everything. Let me do this for you. Let me ease the damn burden you put on yourself. Why do you think I did all this anyway? It was for you and Quinn. To make sure that you would always be taken care of."

"I appreciate that Mason, I do. I just… I want to make my own way. I don't want to rely on you or anyone else. I want to work. I want to be a physical therapist and work with athletes. I didn't go through all this schooling for nothing."

"Then work for me." While I find the humor in his suggestion, he does not. The look on his face serious, no humor in his eyes. "I mean it. Be my own personal trainer. You've been doing amazing things with my…"

"I'm glad. But come on, you know as well as I do it's the same thing as you just paying my way. I can't do that."

"Fine. Can we at least agree that you will live here free and clear?"

"Mason…"

"Oh, come on. The place is already paid off. What the hell would the purpose of paying me anything even be?"

"Fine. No rent. But…"

"But what?"

Crawling into his lap, I smile. "What if I offered you something non-monetary?"

"Such as?"

My lips press against his neck. "How about two blow jobs a week?"

My hands slide into his shorts.

"I think that sounds… fair."

"How about I make my first installment now?" I ask as I slide down his body.

Chapter 32

Mason

It's my first day back at practice. Luckily, Trent is still suspended due to the investigation surrounding his involvement. I'm not sure if I could handle facing him right now, let alone practicing with him. Avery's certain it was him, and I'm more than inclined to believe her.

"What's on the agenda tonight?" Avery asks. She's still in bed as I finish getting dressed for practice. The sheet is pulled up around her, and it takes every bit of strength that I have not to rid her of it and skip practice altogether.

"Dinner and a movie sound good?" I ask. Avery nods her head. The idea of staying in and being together, just the two of us, is very appealing after the past couple of weeks. "Any particular movie?"

"How about a romantic comedy?" she suggests.

"Action movie."

"Drama."

"Superhero."

"Captain America," she states with a smile.

"No way in hell am I going to sit there while you drool all over that guy," I argue.

We continue on this path until it's time for me to leave. "Be back soon," I tell her as I press a kiss to her forehead. One brush of my lips against hers would mean that my ass wouldn't be going to practice. I would end up in bed. In her.

And fuck if that doesn't sound a whole hell of a lot more appealing.

I take one last look at her and marvel at how I got so damn lucky before heading out the door to leave for practice.

Everything finally feels like it's falling into place. I've got the perfect girl. I've got my career. Everything is perfect.

At least for a moment.

When I step out of my apartment building, the last thing that I expect to see is the man standing before me. Eyes that are just like mine, only older and tired, looking stare back at me. It's like looking in a twisted mirror. One that has me remembering exactly who he is and how much alike we really are. The sight of him alone puts me on edge.

"What are you doing back in town?" I ask.

"Business."

"Business?" I let out a hearty laugh. "You've never even held down a job. What the fuck kind of business could you possibly have?"

There's an evil smile on his face as he continues to stare at me but never answers my question.

"So much for that sparkling career," he says.

The fucker has never had a dime to his name. If he did, he sure as hell never used it to take care of his children. And now he's standing here in the doorway of my high-rise condo, insulting me?

I take a step closer to him, my feet heavy against the pavement, my hands clenching at my sides. My body towers over his. There was a time when he seemed so much bigger, so much more powerful. He terrified me. And now?

Now I literally have to restrain myself from ripping him apart. My size, my strength, he's no match for it. Not even close. I would pulverize him. And I want to. I want to so fucking much that I can taste it.

There's too much at stake now, too much to lose.

"Screw you," I say.

"Is that any way to talk to your father? Your mentor?"

"You're no father. Certainly not mine."

There's a subtle shake of his head, then a hearty laugh. "Oh, please, kid, you and me, we're more alike than you know. Remember that time we went to the strip club? You were what? Fourteen, maybe?"

I try to push the memory his words bring up out of my head. The strip club. My fourteenth birthday. The night I lost my virginity to some girl that most definitely shouldn't have been in that club. The one that was too eager to please despite her young age.

Just like that, it all comes flooding back. The strip club was only the start. They didn't want kids; they wanted employees. They wanted to turn us into them. No way would I let that happen to Q, not to my baby sister. So, I did it. I followed in his footsteps in order to be able to protect her. Became the son he wanted me to be – anything to make sure Quinn was safe.

Until I met Coach. Until he pushed them away and helped me get into Remington University. Coach is my real father. Not the man standing before me.

"I am nothing like you," I argue, regurgitating the words that Avery has drilled in my head over the last several weeks. I don't say them for his benefit, but rather for mine. A way to remind myself that I'm not him. That I would never be like him.

"Believe what you want, kid, but we both know the apple doesn't fall far from the tree." There's the slightest bit of pride in his eyes. "You run through pussy like most people drink water. Until you fucked up and started dating that Avery girl."

"Don't you say her name," I warn him.

I don't give a damn what he says or what he thinks about me. Her name doesn't need to be falling from his lips.

"Why the hell would you give up all that ass for her? You knock the little slut up or something?"

He's goading me, and despite the fact that I know it, I eat it right up. I fall into his little trap.

My hands fist in his shirt, and I slam him against the glass wall of the building. "Watch your fucking mouth. I will not let you talk about her like that. Avery is…"

"Too good for you?"

This time, I don't argue. He's right. Avery is good and kind. She's sweet. Innocent.

"You keep going with her, and she'll turn out just like your mom did. Taking drugs, fucking men while I watch. Turning tr…."

My ears begin to ring, drowning out the sound of his voice. Visions of Avery broken and hurt filling my mind. If I hurt her again if I fuck up…. What happens to her? What will become of her?

Everything I so desperately tried to protect her from, myself included, will destroy her.

No. She deserves better than that. Better than me. She deserves someone who isn't tainted like I am. Broken.

Just like I knew. Just like I've always known.

I was kidding myself thinking it could be more. That I could be more.

The past that I'll never be able to escape. The memories that I will never be able to overcome. I hurt her, just like all the others. I used her for sex, just like I did them.

I let him go. I back away.

"Stay away from me. Stay away from my family."

"Or what?" he taunts me.

"I will kill you with my bare hands."

As he begins to laugh, my eyes gravitate to the phone in his hand. The screen lit up; the record button highlighted. Fucking hell.

I threatened him. Told him I would kill him, and he's got it all on tape.

I just destroyed everything in my life in one swoop.

"Get the fuck out of here," I shout at him.

"Happily. I got what I needed."

226

226

Chapter226

Chapter 33226

Chapter 33

Chapter 33

226

Chapter 33226

Chapter 33

Avery226

Chapter 33

Avery226

Chapter 33

Avery226

Chapter 33

Avery226

Chapter 33

Avery226

Chapter 33

Avery226

Chapter 33

Avery

minutes ago, you walked out of here telling me you loved me and couldn't wait for our night together. What changed?"

"Jesus, Avery, what do you want me to say? I don't love you? Because I don't. I don't want a relationship? You already knew that."

I pick up the bag he's packing and throw it across the room. "Screw you, Mason. You know what the real problem is? You're a coward."

"I was when I agreed to pursue something with you. I did it because it's what you wanted, not what I wanted."

I laugh. A ridiculous, insane laugh. "Do you even hear yourself? I only told you how I felt. I never asked for anything in return. You. You were the one who moved me in here, professed your love. You did this. Not me."

A war wages inside me. Do I stay and fight him? Or do I give up and leave?

He's pushing me away rather than pulling me in like he usually does. That means that whatever this is – it's bad.

"Talk to me, Mason." I don't know what else to do but keep trying. Plead with him. Beg him. Fuck him if that's what it takes to get his emotions in check and get him to talk to me. When he doesn't respond, I continue. "Tell me what's happening. Because something isn't right. Something is wrong. You told me you don't want to lose me."

"I don't want to date you either," he deadpans.

"Fine."

"Fine?" he laughs as he follows me to the front door.

"Yes, Mason, fine. You can have it your way. You can push me away and try to destroy your life – for now. Once you pull your head out of your ass – call me because as much as I hate this outburst. As much as I hate what you're doing right now, I know it's not real. I know it's because you're scared and hurting. So, do whatever you need to do. I'll be at home. Waiting."

"Waiting for what?"

I close the gap between us, my hand gently caressing his cheek. "For you to remember that you aren't him. And for you to realize that we're inevitable."

My lips press a chaste kiss to his before walking out the door.

Somehow, I managed to hold it together. Somehow, I managed to stay strong and not fall apart. But the minute the elevator door closes, I collapse to the floor. The tears I had been holding back spillover. I take the elevator ride to the lobby. The few moments are all I allow myself in order to pull it together. I have to believe I'm right. I have to believe that something happened to cause this abrupt change. Because we can't be over. Not when we just started.

Chapter 34

Mason

"What do you mean, it's over?" Lou asks. Coach Reed is standing next to him, his hand scrubbing over his face.

"I mean, exactly what I said. Avery and I ended things."

Lou shakes his head. "She can't do that. We have a contract."

"She didn't do anything. And you're going to let her out of that contract."

"Like hell we are," Lou shouts. "You were just…"

I sit in the seat across from where he's standing and cross my arms. "Just what, Lou?"

"Not looking like such as asshole," he says.

"Fooled you," I laugh. Sitting up straighter in the chair, I rest my elbows on the mahogany conference table. "Listen, I promise I will continue to be on my best behavior. Even without Avery. This is for the best."

"For, who? You? So, you can get your dick wet again?" Coach chimes in.

Little does he know my dick was more than satisfied with all the things Avery could do to it.

"There's nothing she can do to help me. Not now."

"What does that mean?"

"I fucked up. Big time," I tell them.

Lou throws his hands up in frustration while Coach just stares at me. Lou cares about the image. Coach, he knows me; he gives a damn about me. At least a little. So, he knows whatever this is, it isn't the usual bullshit I would pull. Especially not if I'm walking away from Avery.

"What did he do?" Coach Red asks.

"Huh?" I ask. His question confusing me.

"Your dad. He was in town, was he not?" I nod my head, unsure how he knew any of that while knowing that he would at the same time.

"He got me to say something stupid. Something damning."

"Like?"

"Like telling him if he set foot near Quinn, I would kill him. And I meant it. I fucking meant it Coach and…"

His hands clamp down on my shoulders and squeeze. "It's okay, kid."

"Okay? It is not okay?" Lou yells as he walks around the room in a state of panic. "This is it. He's over. It's done. My career is ruined."

"Who put him up to it?" Coach asks, ignoring the tirade that Lou is on.

"I don't know. He wouldn't tell me."

"I'll take care of it." Coach's voice is confident. Too confident. I remember him saying the same words to me when I first signed with the team, and my dad tried to extort money from me.

"What did you do?" I ask him as I turn my head in his direction.

"Nothing, yet."

"No, when I first signed with the Red Devils. You did something to make him go away then, too. What did you do?"

Red smiles. "Nothing to worry that pretty little playboy head of yours over." He begins to walk away, then stops and turns back to me. "This why you ended things with Avery?"

My gaze drops to my hands.

Coach's shoulders sag. "Mason…"

"Don't. Okay? I don't want to hear it."

"Well, that's just too damn bad." He presses his palms to the table and leans toward me. "You aren't him, son. In fact, you're nothing like him. I know that Quinn knows that. And Avery? She knew that before anyone. It's why she puts up with your sorry ass. It's why she loves you."

I glance up at Red. "She shouldn't."

"No, you're right, she shouldn't. But she does. And you pushing her away because you're scared – it's not going to change that."

Chapter 35

Mason

The locker on the opposite side of the room from mine is empty. The very one that usually houses Trent's gear. I secretly pray that he got traded, but when I see Coach walk into the locker room, I know there is more to it.

He nods his head in the direction of his office.

I follow him inside, and he closes the door behind us. "I want you to hear this from me. Take a seat."

Doing as he asks, I sit in the chair directly across from his. "Hear what?"

"I met with your father," Coach tells me.

"And?"

"It seems like your dad was working for Trent," Coach tells me. "When his little ploy with Avery didn't work, he started looking for other weaknesses. Somehow, he found your dad, offered him a shit ton of money to fuck with your head and destroy you. He's the one that shot Avery. He's the one that…"

It can't be. I couldn't have heard him right. My father shot Avery? He tried to take away the only good thing in my life? Hadn't he already taken enough? Destroyed me enough?

I'm going to kill him.

It's the only thing I am thinking as I spring out of the chair and head for the door that Coach has now stepped in front of.

"Sit your ass down," he tells me. "You going out there and killing him isn't going to do anyone any good. Besides…" There's a smile on Coach's face. "I already punched his sorry ass for you. Right before I called the police and had him arrested."

"He's in jail?"

Coach nods. "The only downside is, they're not arresting Trent. However, it was enough for the organization to release him. He's off the team, Mase."

It's not much of a consolation, but it's something.

"Why? Why in the hell was he so dead set on destroying me?" I ask, still trying to figure out what in the hell Trent has against me.

"It's not a good reason by any means," Coach says. "But one that I think you'll understand."

What the fuck, is he talking in code now? "Just tell me."

"Apparently, back in college, you uh… you fucked his girlfriend, Mason. And what started out as him wanting to pay you back for that with Avery turned into so much more."

Running my hands through my hair, I can't seem to help myself – I laugh. "I screwed around a lot in college, Coach, but never with anyone who was taken. It's not my style."

Not after how I grew up. Not after the things I saw. I would never ruin someone's life like that. Destroy a relationship or marriage? Never.

"Seems like he should have been more pissed at her than you."

"Or she was lying."

It doesn't matter anymore. Nothing I did warrants the extent that he went to. Having Avery shot? Hiring my dad to do it?

The guy is fucking crazy, obviously.

"That's it? It's over?"

Coach smiles. "It's over, Mase. Go get your girl. Go celebrate."

"I already told you, Avery and I are over. It's better this way."

"Like hell it is, kid. You and that girl, you're meant to be. Quit being an idiot – or I'll bench your ass."

He's only fucking with me, I know that. As much as I want to believe that we're meant to be, the thing I believe wholeheartedly is that Avery deserves a better life than I can give her.

Chapter 36

Avery

I sort through the dresses in my closet. The clothing that I had Quinn retrieve from Mason's condo. Not because I feared going there. Not because I didn't want to see him – I do. God, do I ever want to see his handsome face and those gorgeous brown eyes. I would love nothing more than to look into them and see the reminder that he does love me. That this little plan that I've devised is not for naught.

One thing Mason can't stand – another man with his hands on me. Not before we were dating, and sure as hell not now. It's the only thing that I can think of to remind him what it is that he feels for me.

That right there is the key word. Feel.

I need to make him feel it because me just telling him isn't going to work. No. He has to feel the emotion, allow everything he is burying deep down to protect himself from any kind of pain to surface. Only then will he be able to open up and tell me what in the hell went wrong.

I refuse to believe that he doesn't want to be with me. Or that the happiness that we shared was all for my benefit. Knowing Mason better than he knows himself, I know that isn't true. I know he loves me. I know he wants to be with me.

Most people would probably say I was a fool and a doormat to let Mason walk all over me like this. But those people don't know. They don't understand. No one fully knows the pain and trauma that Mason went through. The things he saw his parents do. Things he desperately sheltered Quinn from. Then to have to be the adult? Be the one responsible for taking care of his younger sister when he himself needed taking care of?

Most don't understand the broken pieces inside Mason.

I do.

And I am willing to do whatever I have to in order to get him to the other side. We were close. So close. Until something set him back.

But what?

Hunter and Quinn seem as clueless as I am.

Where they can't help him, I can.

"Woah, are you seriously planning on wearing that?" Quinn asks as she eyes the dress I'm holding in my hands.

Black. Mason's favorite color. Short. So short, Mason will be able to see nearly every inch of his favorite body part – my legs. Sequins so I shine and catch attention – his.

Billy Saint generously agreed to play the role of my admirer tonight. He thinks we're just playing a joke on Mason. One of his favorite things to do. Little does he know how insane this is going to drive him. Small price to pay for getting us straightened out.

Hunter will be picking up Mason, bringing him to the club under the guise of trying to make him feel better. I, however, fully intend on making him feel worse. Let's just hope my acting skills are up to the challenge. How I am supposed to look happy and like I'm having the time of my life when my heart is in shambles, I don't know. It's not like when I was faking being Mason's girlfriend. That was easy. That felt real. It was real. This…

This is one hundred percent not real. It is necessary, though.

The only way to get Mason to pull his head out of his ass.

"Yep."

"Where in the hell did you get that?" she asks, surprised that me and my much more conservative style would have something like this.

"I…uh… I may have stolen it from you," I say sheepishly.

Quinn yanks the dress from my hand and twirls it. "Good choice. This is going to make my brother's eyes fall out of their sockets."

"That's the plan."

Well, that, and to piss him off. Throwing him into a jealous rage is going to be the easy part. The hard part is going to be getting him to admit why. Getting him to open up and tell me what in the hell is going on? Part of me worries that even this dress, even the very sexy Billy Saint, won't break him.

It has to. This has to work. Because if it doesn't? I'm out of options.

"You okay?" Quinn asks as she helps me put the finishing touches on. Hair up, earrings in, make-up subtly sexy.

"I'm nervous," I admit.

"About what? This is going to work like a charm," she says, tucking in a strand of my hair.

"What if it doesn't though?" Quinn begins to protest, but I cut her off. "I mean it. If this doesn't work…"

"Then you move on," she deadpans. She says it like it's the easiest thing in the world.

"It's not that easy."

"I didn't say it would be easy, but what other choice would you have? Sit around and wait for Mason to finally get his head out of his ass? No, I don't think so. You are better than that. No, what you would do is take that job across the country and make a life for yourself. Forget about Mason, hell forget about Remington. Just not me, okay?"

I give her hand a gentle squeeze. "I could never forget you."

Just like I would never be able to forget Mason either.

"Besides, I fully intend on us having fun tonight," Quinn tells me just as Claire enters the room.

"Pre-game anyone?" she asks.

"Um, there are only two drinks," I say.

"Yeah, they're both for you. I thought you might need them," Claire tells me with a laugh.

I take a glass from her hand and drink it. Then the next.

"Better?" she asks.

"Better." Not great. But definitely better.

"Let's roll," Quinn cheers as she ushers us out of the apartment.

We arrive at the club, and Mason is nowhere in sight. They should be here in about thirty minutes if

Hunter's text was accurate. Billy is here, and he's already a little tipsy. And handsy.

"You're going to have to do a better job than that," I laugh, his arm around my shoulder and his hand resting on my boob.

"What? Isn't this how Mason would do it?" he teases.

"No, he would just put her on top of the bar and…"

"Quinn!" I exclaim.

"What? You think I didn't hear you two in your room when…."

"Enough," I order her.

My cheeks are burning; I can feel them flush to what I am sure is a bright red.

"Naughty girl," Billy teases.

"Stop it, both of you," I tell them.

"Here we go," Claire says, nodding her head in the direction of the entrance where Mason and Hunter are walking in.

It's now or never.

Chapter 37

Mason

"Why in the hell did you bring me here?" I ask Hunter.

We're standing in the VIP section of some club that's filled with mostly college students. At one point in time, yes, I would have loved it here. My dick and I would have taken advantage of every opportunity this place provides. And believe me, there were always plenty.

"I thought you could use a night out. Relax a little."

"You hate places like this," I tell him. The guy bitched and moaned more times than I can count when I would drag him to places just like this. Now, with Quinn in the picture, he expects me to believe he wants to be here.

"I do," he agrees. "Especially knowing I have Quinn waiting for me at home. This isn't about me. It's about you. You went from self-destructing to not existing. You need to find a happy medium."

For a short while, I had. Avery was my happy medium. Hell, she was my happy place.

"I don't feel like being happy," I say between clenched teeth.

"Yeah, well, you need to do something because you're pissing everyone on the team off."

"Fuck them."

"You're not my type, Adams," Ashton says as he approaches Hunter and me.

"Being the new kid, you sure as hell have a lot of balls," I tell him taking a step forward. I like the guy, but right now with the mood I'm in, I don't feel up to dealing with his shit.

Hunter puts his hand to my chest and presses me back. "Relax, Mase, he's just messing with you."

Honestly, I don't give a fuck if he's messing with me or actually being a prick. All I want to do is go home to wallow in self-pity. Is that too much to fucking ask for?

I throw back another drink. As I set the glass down, my eyes catch a glimpse of brown hair piled up on top of a woman's head. Her neck is long, sleek. The sight makes my cock twitch and my heart ache.

"Did you know she was going to be here?" I shout at Hunter. Of course, he knew. Because standing next to Avery is Quinn. "This was a fucking set-up."

"No shit," Ashton says with a laugh.

"Shut it," I warn him. His hands raise in surrender. My attention back on Hunter, "Why the fuck would you do this?"

"Because you needed a reminder," he deadpans.

"A reminder of what?" I argue.

As far as I can tell, I don't need any reminders of what I'm missing out on or what I could have had. I know it all too well.

Just like I know that I can never give her what she deserves. I wish like hell that I could, but I can't. I'm too broken. Too much like him to risk it.

There's a guy standing next to Avery. Not just any guy either. Billy fucking Saint. The prick. What the fuck is he doing back in town? Better yet, what the fuck is he doing with his arm around Avery?

Billy moves in, nuzzling Avery's neck. The smile on her face is instant, and it infuriates me. I know that smile. I've seen it before, directed at me. She's interested. Maybe not in him, maybe just in what he can provide her. A temporary distraction. Because we might be over, but I know for certain that the feelings haven't gone away. Not for either of us.

"I can't watch this," I say, slamming back another drink. "I'm out of here."

Hunter steps in front of me. "Like hell you are."

"Don't make me fight you," I say as I stand up taller. I puff my chest out, ready to fight.

"You know what I can't watch? You fucking destroy the best thing that's ever happened to you, that's what." Hunters hand press against my chest and shove me back. "Get him out of your head. Get him out of your mind. You. Are. Not. Him."

There's only one way he knows. "Did he get to her?" I ask, terrified that my sister had to look into the face of that man like I did.

"No, of course not," Hunter replies. "I would never let that happen. I hate that he got to you." His hands are on his waist, his head hung. "I know it was hard seeing him. I know it was tough to have all that old shit stirred up. But you know that's what they wanted, right?"

They. Trent, his agent – my dad. They pulled out every damn stop to destroy me. First Avery in that shooting. Then throwing my dad in my face. It's all been one big fucking shit storm meant to screw with my head. I'll be damned if it didn't work like a fucking charm.

"It doesn't matter. It...." I catch a glimpse of Billy sliding his arm around Avery, tucking her closer against him. Fuck. "This was a bad idea, Hunter."

So many bad thoughts are running through my head. So much anger coursing through my veins. And the only person I want to take it out on? The guy with his hands on Avery – Billy.

"A really bad idea," I say as I walk out of our VIP area and straight toward Avery.

"Mason," she says. Her eyes say she's surprised by my presence; her body screams that she's ready for a fight. Avery moves out of Billy's hold and steps toward me. "What are you doing here?"

I might be looking at her, but I'm speaking to him. "Keep your hands off her," I say to him. Not that he looks phased in the slightest by my warning. In fact, he's standing there looking like a smug prick.

"Why should he?" Avery chimes in. "You don't want your hands on me. Why shouldn't he?"

"You know that's not true," I say somberly.

"You're right; I do. But I also know that you're acting like a child. You're letting some asshole from your past dictate our future."

"It's more than that," I say, trying to explain. The music is so loud I can barely hear myself.

"Bullshit, Mason. I call bullshit. You're giving him control. You're letting him affect you now when you never did before. So, what's different now? Hmm?"

I don't answer; I just drop my gaze to the floor.

"That's what I thought. Good-night, Mason."

When I look up at her, she's taking Billy's hand and nodding in the direction of the exit. As they head toward the door, my feet are cemented to the ground.

A war wages in my head. Do I go after her? Or do I let her go? Let her find her happily ever after?

I charge for the door, following them into the street.

"You. You're what's different," I yell into the night.

"You're blaming this on me?" she asks incredulously.

"No. And it's not some weak ass attempt at an excuse, either. It's the truth. You make this whole thing different. If it was anyone else..." I shake my head. "I never wanted more until I realized that I wanted you. And seeing my dad again..."

"You saw your dad?"

All I can do is nod. Because I don't want to tell her the things he said or that they're the reason I put us in this position.

"Is that what all this is about?" she asks. She leaves new guy in the dust and meets me where I stand in the middle of the street. "You're not him. Not even close."

"We don't know that. He wasn't always like he was either. I've hurt you enough. I won't risk doing it again."

Her hand touches my cheek. "Don't you know that the thing that hurts me the most is not being with you? I love you, Mason. Every screwed up piece. Because let's face it, we're both a little fucked up. That's what makes us so perfect. We understand each other's broken pieces. We accept them."

For the first time since she approached me, I touch her. I need to feel her, to feel that connection that we share.

"You've never hurt me, Mason. Not like that. And there isn't a doubt in my mind – you never would."

"I'm scared, Ave. I'm so scared of becoming him. Of hurting you."

"Who he is – that's a choice he made. He chose the drugs, the sex, and whatever else they were into. You? You chose to fight. You chose to work hard and become someone. You chose not to be anything like him."

"I chose you. I tried to be a man worthy of you – of your friendship."

She presses her lips to mine. "And you always will be. Because that, Mason Ford, is who you are."

"You're not going to let me walk away, are you?"

"Are you kidding me? Who do you think came up with this whole plan?" She's smiling, looking smug at her knowledge of me and how to use it against me.

"You played me," I say.

She shrugs. "You're done playing the field, Mason. I'm the only teammate you need."

"You're the only one I want," I smile back.

This time when we kiss, I don't stop. My arms wrap around her, our lips crash together, tongues dancing to a familiar beat.

Avery McCoy is the only damn touchdown I care about making.

Epilogue

Avery

I walk into Coach Reed's office. The call from him was unexpected, and despite his plea to see me in person, I'm still not exactly sure what this is all about.

Trent left the Red Devils, and from what I hear, no one else wants him after the shit he pulled with Mason.

Mason, on the other hand, is on top of his game. Both on and off the field.

We're happier than I ever could have imagined, he's getting the help that he needs though he would never admit that to anyone but me, and on the field, he's playing like never before. Personally, I think it's having this weight lifted off his shoulders. The therapy he's completing and his ability to now deal with his childhood, or lack thereof, and the fact that he is nothing like his father is making him more whole. A complete man. Finally, after years of fearing becoming his father, of hurting those that he loves, he's free.

I wish it hadn't taken us what it did to get here, but I wouldn't change a thing. We are who we are. We lived the childhoods that we did, and we persevered. Most importantly, we did it together. Sure, there were bumps in the road, and for a while there, goddamn mountains, too.

"Hey, Coach, you wanted to see me?" I ask as I step into his office.

He's seated at his desk, Mason across from him. My eyes dart between the two and the mischievous smiles they have on their faces, and I wonder what they're up to.

"Should I be worried?" I ask.

"This is me, Aves. You really think you have to worry about anything where I'm involved?" Mason asks.

My reply? A resounding yes.

The man is trouble. In the best kind of way, but trouble, nonetheless. Between that look in his eyes and the smile on his face, I know he's up to something.

"Have a seat," Coach tells me.

Out of respect, I do as he says. But I'm still on guard.

"Will someone please tell me what's going on already?" I ask impatiently. The wait is killing me.

"Mason mentioned that you had a job lined up in New York but opted to stay here in Remington to be with him," Coach says.

I nod my head. It wasn't a difficult choice to make. Sure, the job would have been amazing. It was exactly what I had hoped to land after college – therapist for a major league sports team. Being with Mason has been the happiest time of my life. We're far from perfect, but we're together. And we're happy. And he loves me. That right there is all I ever dreamed of.

"Not sure why you put up with his ass, but I'm glad you do. You make him a better man," Coach tells me.

"He made me the better person," I argue. Because if not for Mason protecting me from my father, getting him out of my life once and for all, who knows where I would be right now.

"Let's agree to disagree on that, hmm?" Coach gives me a smile. "Anyway, Mason feels terrible that you gave everything up for him. He asked me if I had any connections somewhere a little closer to home."

I can feel the excitement bubble inside of me. Coach has connections everywhere. And if they called me here, it has to be for something, right? Maybe the Remington Wreckers baseball team needs a therapist. Or the hockey team. Shit, what are they called again?

"Ave?" Mason's voice breaks through my giddy thoughts.

"Yeah, sorry. You were saying?"

"I told him I could do him one better. I would love to offer you a position here, with the Red Devils."

Feeling like a cartoon character whose jaw just hit the floor, I pull myself together and manage to say, "What?"

"We have an open position, and I want you to fill it. What do you say?" Coach asks.

I glance over at Mason, who is beaming and fully believe he had more to do with this than Coach is letting on.

"I don't know what to say," I stammer.

Mason leans over, his shoulder bumping into mine. "How about, yes?"

"Yes, of course," I shout out in excitement. "I can't believe… I don't know… thank you."

"No need to thank me," Coach says, giving a nod in Mason's direction. "He can be pretty persuasive."

"Believe me, I know," I reply. I'm smiling like a fool and trying to contain my excitement by not jumping into Mason's lap and kissing the breath out of him.

"Well, now that that is settled, what do you say we go celebrate?" Mason stands and extends his hand to me, which I happily take.

"You want to come, Coach?" I ask just before Mason wraps his arms around my waist to drag me away.

"Nah," Coach replies with a wave of his hand. "You kids go and have fun."

I thank him again just before Mason shuts the door behind us.

"What's the rush?" I ask.

The wicked smile on his face tells me all I need to know. He's eagerly anticipating his "thank you."

"Just want to celebrate. You get your dream job, I get my girl, and we can live happily ever after. If you want to, that is."

"What do you mean, if I want to?" I say with a laugh.

Mason stops in front of the Red Devils sign and turns to me. "I mean, I want us to have a real happily ever after." I'm about to question him again when he drops to one knee.

"What in the hell are you doing?" I ask as I stare down in disbelief. Before me, on his knees, is a man who never wanted love or commitment but is now about to make the ultimate one. I'm confused and thrilled and baffled as I stare at him in wonderment. My knees become weak, and my heart begins to race as I realize that this moment is really happening in the most Mason kind of way — spontaneous.

"If you would shut up for a minute, I am trying to propose to you."

I shake my head, unwilling to accept the truth that I see in his eyes or the words that he utters from those gorgeous lips.

"This is real, Ave. Me and you? We've always been real. I was just too stupid to see it."

"This is a huge step," I say.

"Is it though? We've spent every day of our lives together. We love each other. We support each other. We fuck like goddamn perfection. This isn't a huge step; it's the right step. The only step. Marry me, Ave. Please?"

"Can I think about it?" I tease him.

"Absolutely not."

"Then I guess I have no choice but say… yes! Always yes!"

SCARLET LANTERN
Publishing

Also Written By L.M. Reid

The Hard to Love Series

Hard to Hate
Hard to Trust
Hard to Forgive

Making the Play Series

Playing the Game
Playing the Field
Playing to Win
Played Out – Coming Soon

About the Author

L.M. Reid is a reader, writer, and lover of all things romance. Just a girl from the Midwest with simple tastes and dirty thoughts. If she's not busy clicking away at her laptop with an iced coffee in hand, she can be found at home surrounded by hot wheels and the love of her husband and son.

Book Bub: http://scarlet.pub/LMBB
Facebook (Page): https://scarlet.pub/LMFB
Instagram: https://scarlet.pub/LMIG
Goodreads: https://scarlet.pub/LMGR

And don't forget to join my reader group:
L.M. Reid's Steamy Romance Readers
https://scarlet.pub/LMGroup